Pistol

Pistol

A Novel by Adrienne Richard

Little, Brown and Company

Boston   Toronto   London

Library of Congress Catalog Card Number 69-17753

10   9   8   7   6
BP

Joy Street Books are published by
Little, Brown and Company (Inc.).

*Published simultaneously in Canada
by Little, Brown & Company (Canada) Limited*
PRINTED IN THE UNITED STATES OF AMERICA

This book was originally for Jim, Dan and Randy, and it still is. Now it is also for Emily, Tylea and Nigel, because it is their grandfather, James E. Richard, who grew up in southeastern Montana and worked as "Pistol" on the ranches there. This book is based on his experiences.

Contents

PART ONE

Sunup

Before Sam's

I

Life began for me and my older brother Conrad in the little town of LeVent on Montana's north-central prairie. The town was named for the wind, and the wind is what I remember. It drove relentlessly, day and night, across the plains. Its nonhuman sound gave a great feeling of loneliness which even a small child detected. At night Conrad and I huddled together in the double bed, listening to the wind's incantations rounding the house. Conrad was mean, and we spent most of our time in fights which I lost, but at night when the wind whined, we stuck together against that unseen foe.

Conrad was three years older than I, a fact he was not disposed to let me forget, and he interfered with my getting the attention I deserved from my mother. I was relieved when Conrad went to school. Then alone together my mother and I made cookies at the kitchen table. Mine were lumpy, gray ones which she covered with colored sugar while we chattered and I amused her. "Oh, are you the charmer!" she laughed, and I laughed, knowing that was a good thing to be. By afternoon, however, the peace and quiet and relief had lasted too long, and I waited at the window for Conrad.

My mother was a small woman whose health and vigor had already begun to fail when I first remember her.

My father was on the tall side, a little under six feet, and thin with long, thin muscles which I often watched as he stood in the bathroom shaving and pulling his chin first to one side, then the other, stripped down to his pants and his white underwear vest. He had hollow cheeks and birdlike eyes too small for his face.

He dispensed discipline in an awesome manner. As I saw it fall on Conrad, I listened to instinct tell me how to avoid it. My father came and went to work daily; he read the weekly paper and *Collier's* magazine and the *Saturday Evening Post* at night; and he carved the Sunday roast in paternal fashion.

One thing I knew, he was a restless man. When LeVent didn't grow much, he got light-footed, as the cowboys say, because my father wanted to get in on the ground floor of something that was going to be big. The little guy had to get in at the start, my father said. So we crisscrossed the state of Montana from one small town to another which he figured was about to start growing. We touched down at Libby in the heart of forest and mountains and lakes where lumber was going to be big, but somehow it didn't pan out and soon we moved on. We hit Shelby just before Jack Dempsey fought Sheriff Gibbons there. My father had bought a carload of binoculars to sell to the crowd. He intended to clean up on the binoculars and with this bonanza get a business of his own. But the crowd got so unruly that they broke down the fences around the boxing ring, and we were lucky to get out of Shelby, leaving the carload of binoculars behind. Next we hit a wheat town on the prairies again where railroad car loadings of grain dropped off right after we got there. We moved on again. We never went to the bigger places, Missoula or Great Falls or Billings. My father stuck to the small towns, but each town was like the last. Its promise petered out, and we moved on until we reached Great Plain when I was eight years old.

Great Plain was the biggest town my father tried, about eight thousand counting grasshoppers and critters, and it straddled the main line of the Northern Pacific railroad. On the north side of the tracks were Main Street and the business district and the churches and the good houses. On the south were dilapidated houses, two-bit stores and the Jehovah's Witness Hall. At the very edge of town were the stockyards, the fences and corrals and pens and loading chutes laid out in a multitude of squares and rectangles which were alive with critters mooing and bellering, to use the cowboy word, night and day. Great Plain was a cow town. It beat with a vitality none of the other towns had. It was a great town for a boy. It had a legendary past with fiction so liberally surrounding the facts that no one knew or cared to know what really happened. It had been buffalo country, the hunting range of Sioux and Cheyenne and part of the domain of the great Crazy Horse and Sitting Bull, and it had quartered the United States Army in its last campaign against the red men. When the Indians had gone, and the railroad reached the

5

town, it grew and found its natural form as a cow town. With the waving rich prairie grass, the plentiful water in the Yellowstone and the Honey rivers and in the little creeks that ran out of the pine hills, the region became cattle country. First came the longhorns that were trailed up from Texas, the legendary great herds a boy can easily imagine, and later came more sedentary men, homesteading ranchers who ran their cattle on the open range with other men's stock, knowing their own by earmarks and hide brands. After them came the fences and men even more settled who confined their critters to their own range, which was the manner of living when we got there.

When the little kids cried, "The Indians are camping out by the fairgrounds," I rode my bicycle to the edge of town to see for myself, and with my heart banging and the bike bar between my legs for a quick getaway I saw them from the discreet side of the street — a man in braids, a woman with a papoose slung in her J. C. Penney blanket, and the little kids who stared back, hugging their dolls close to them. I marveled at the height and spread of the great canvas tepees set like cones on the empty prairie. When the dogs slunk toward me snarling and slobbering, my feet hit the pedals and my legs pumped frantically until I was blocks away in friendly territory again.

Not that I was scared of Indians. Just the opposite. The first day in the new school a black-haired kid named Richie Greatbear had befriended me. He was part Cheyenne, different and kind of magical, and the tagalongs followed Richie so that I missed out on a lot of trouble. Later on he cut his finger. I picked a scab off my elbow. We mixed our blood in a bottle cap, and each took a lick. That made us blood brothers, and afterwards, he called me Cat and I called him Bear.

When the fall drive came in, the bawling and bellering and the smell of cattle drifted over the whole town. We biked in droves down to the stockyards to watch. Conrad and I climbed to the top rail and watched the cowboys work the gates and the commission men size up the stock and the buyers and sellers make parlay at the scales. There I saw Seth McCollum for the first time, and Conrad whispered, "He was a rustler once," and I was filled with awe. Naturally I believed him. Any man that old, it was reasonable.

For all its vitality, its history and zest, Great Plain didn't grow much, and we might have left there if my mother hadn't set herself against it. At the supper table when my father was coming out with the next move, he'd heard, he said, that . . . but he got no farther. My mother burst into tears and said she wouldn't budge, she was staying right here, and he could go anywhere he liked. My father was the maddest I'd ever seen him. I don't think she stood up to him very often, but this time she won.

In short order I forgot all about it. I got my paper route. It wasn't a neighborhood route. My territory was both sides of the main street in the middle of town. For me it was perfect. While the other kids stuffed their papers into bags over the rear tire and biked off in all directions, I had left for the Laurel Hotel where I peddled to the salesmen sitting around the lobby in leather armchairs. Every one of them was good for a sale. Then out the front veranda past the split hickory rockers where the commercial travelers sat on summer nights and up the street, working the shops and Acton's drugstore and the people on the street until I came to the saddle shop. I didn't spend much time in the store part but went through to the back and upstairs to the big loft room which was the workshop. Before I got off the top step, the smell of sawdust and cigarette smoke and hemp rope and heavy leather flooded me. Half a dozen men worked there all the time, building saddles to measure because saddles from that shop were famous all over that part of the West. The men would stop as I came along the benches and worktables and say, "Howdy, Billy, sure I'll take one, we run out of catalogs at my place." In the winter I warmed myself by the fuel oil stove at one end of the workshop just to keep breathing that smell of hemp and leather, and in the summer I lingered in the stifling heat just for the fun of it.

On the other side of the street I sold to Mr. Goldstein, who had a jewelry and pawn shop and signs in his window that read SADDLES LIKE NEW and FOLD BACK CORONA TYPEWRITER VERY REASONABLE, before going on to the Chinaman's cafe and the Plainsman bar.

There the bartender met me at the door and took some papers and brought back the money. I waited inside the door before a colored glass and mahogany partition and patted the moth-eaten back of a stuffed mountain sheep. Then one evening in a blizzard he let me inside, and I sold my papers to the cowboys and a few women in the U-shaped black-leather booths with the tables in the middle. The bartender fixed me up with a drink of hot water and whisky, and I stood at the great bar with my foot on the brass rail and looked secretly into the back room where four men played poker in a green cone of light.

Then I hit the Marshall House on the corner for my last stop, drank a Green River in Acton's soda fountain, and went home. The route meant more than money to me. Here I learned what men and women did outside the snug, coal-hot houses.

Every night my family gathered together at supper. We ate in the kitchen at a big round table always covered with a tablecloth. My father made us stand behind the straight, hard oak chairs until my mother had put all the serving bowls on the table. Then he said, "Conrad, seat your lady mother," and Conrad pulled back her chair for her, and we all sat down, said grace, and fell to it.

After dinner Conrad and I did the dishes, although my mother would just as soon have done them herself. We broke plates; we busted up in a Dutch pile on the kitchen floor with Conrad on top; we forgot the roaster and anything else that looked like work. But my father made her sit in the living room and listen to the Atwater Kent radio and forced us to "build character."

While I explored the life of the town, Conrad worked in the wool house. My father was manager there, and he made Conrad work inside after school and Saturdays and half days in the summer, and Conrad hated it, hated everything about it. His job made my paper route seem even better than it was, a fact I had to rub in from time to time. There aren't many ways to get even with older brothers. I told him how I got a whisky and hot water from the bartender. Conrad gave me a long and terrifying lecture on alcoholism embellished with portraits of various rummy cowboys we saw on the streets, but he never squealed on me. Conrad had some good points.

He could have ended my career as a paper boy with one little word.

Most of the time Conrad was in trouble at home, and in the kitchen after dinner he passed it on. "Boy, you just sit there with that sticky syrup smile on your little round angelic face and say, yes, please, and good dinner, Mom, and all that crap," he whispered over the sink, "and when I don't smile pretty and chirp, then I get it for practically nothing." Conrad was about half right, because I learned a lot just looking at his long, lean face and the chip on his shoulder across the dinner table, but he was no more than half right. When he said practically nothing, he didn't mention that his friends were the toughest kids in town and the mayhem they contrived could only be practiced on the open prairie in a very empty land.

He smirked the sweet smile of revenge on me when he brought his report card home. Conrad's record was brilliant, and mine was mediocre. I didn't dislike school and I didn't find the teachers too bad, but what lay between the book covers struck me as incredibly meager compared to the life around me. The kids at school, Sonny Goldstein, Richie Greatbear, Hack Davis, Raf Gomez, the people and punchers and activity on Main Street, Saturday afternoon at the Lon Chaney thriller enhanced with subtitles, a tin-pan piano and my own imagination, these stirred and fascinated me. There were no dead words to surpass the life I knew.

Each spring my father picked up a couple of old saddle horses cheap down at the stockyards, and Conrad and I staked them out in the piece of vacant prairie called a lot next door. All summer we played cowboy. We rode out on the prairie and roped sagebrush until we roped like old hands. We rode bareback or cinched up the saddles to make the horses buck so that we could learn how to ride buckers, and we knew everything about the prairie. The highest ridges, Signal Butte, Angel Wings, Camelback, the flats where the Honey met the Yellowstone, all the draws and coulees and low places we knew by heart. With the other kids we rode out to the fairgrounds on the Fourth of July to see the rodeo. We got in free, by riding through the contestants' entrance, and tied our horses to the hitching rack behind the bucking chutes and heard the cowboys cussing their luck for a bad ride or an unfair draw and watched the bottle go around behind the judges' stand. We sat on the top rail in the blazing sun all afternoon and watched the calf roping and the team tying which some rodeo rider from Arizona almost always won. Those Arizona boys sure can rope, but when it comes to riding the buckers, take a Montanan every time, so the saying went, and naturally I believed it. The broncs were next to wild and right off the range, and some jumble-brained buster from Ismay was likely to win. It was the most thrilling day of the year, and as we rode homeward, Conrad said, "If I ever get out of the wool house, I'm going to be a cowboy."

"Me, too," I said.

"I mean a real rancher," he said.

"Me, too," I said.

"Don't you ever think of anything for yourself?" he hissed.

Conrad was full of bitterness and disgust. Maybe the wool house did it to him. In cow country it was degrading to have anything to do with sheep. One night he told my father that he was quitting at the wool house because he wanted to go out for high school football. My father was furious and refused. The battle raged until my mother wept. My father yelled at the top of his voice, and Conrad yelled, "But I want to, I want to, that's why." That night he cried bitter tears into the dishpan, because there was no way out. He had to have the signature of parent or guardian on the white permission card, and he wasn't going to get it. From the scared, sick, elated feeling in my stomach I knew I had witnessed something important put to death.

"Why'd you have to tell him that way?" I whispered. "You could have kept your mouth shut and asked Mom. She would've signed it."

"Why didn't you stick up for me?"

I felt horribly guilty. I should have gone to bat for Conrad; I should have stuck up for him; but I hadn't and I knew why. If he got permission for football, then I would get the wool house and I would lose everything. So I kept my mouth shut and didn't stick up for Conrad, sick though it made me with disgust for myself.

Then the unexpected happened. My father came home to dinner obviously agitated. We gathered around, standing behind the solid oak chairs until he said, "Seat your lady mother, Conrad," and we all sat down and mumbled grace and dived in. Against the clatter of big spoons on serving bowls, my father said, "Well, Adelaide, I am leaving the wool house."

The noise cut off like a slice.

My mother said, "We aren't moving!"

"No, we aren't moving," my father said. "There's going to be a meat-packing plant in this town, and I am head of it." We began serving ourselves again, wondering, was that all? but he looked so pleased that I said,

"Gee that's really keen, Dad," as I filled my plate. Conrad didn't say anything. He waited two days and got my mother to sign the permission slip for football.

When my father said meat-packing, I immediately saw cattle, and when I found out he meant horsemeat, the wild horses rounded up and driven off the range, I was filled with horror and disgust. Still, the grass was needed for running critters, I knew that. In my head I knew it. In my heart I bled for the wild mavericks running on the distant ridges, their broomtails streaming behind them in the unremitting wind.

The great ranch country which surrounded my town made up its life. The ranches sustained the town, and the town supplied the ranches. The two were knit together in a common course. There were few boys in town who didn't want to be cowboys, and one by one as they reached thirteen or fourteen, they went out someplace to ride for an uncle or a family friend, and the riding and roping and hanging around the stockpens and watching the annual rodeo we all had done came to good use.

Sam's Place

2

Uncomfortably aware of my now familiar mixture of admiration and envy I helped Conrad pack his duffle one early summer night before he went out to ride for the Kincaid Cattle Company. Kincaid's was the biggest outfit in that region. It ran for twenty-six miles on either side of the Honey River near the Dakota border, and it was an honor to be taken on by the Kincaid brothers. I wondered who would take me.

The Christmas that I was thirteen, I used my paper route money to buy a man-sized saddle which was a little big, but I figured I'd grow. I wanted to be ready if a ranch job came my way.

One night at dinner my father said, "I saw Sam Tolliver today. He's looking for a horse wrangler for the summer. I told him you might be interested, Billy."

My mother was thrilled. "Oh, aren't you lucky! He's such a nice man."

Immediately Conrad knocked the Tolliver ranch as

small-time, nothing to compare to Kincaid's which was a corporation.

I pretended that didn't hurt and told my father I sure was interested, and he made arrangements. I gave my paper route to Richie Greatbear and said so long to Sonny Goldstein and Hack Davis, who next to Richie were my closest friends. The day after school let out, my father drove me out to Sam's.

My father had his own reasons for going that day. All the wild horses on Sam's range had been rounded up for auction, and the horsemeat buyers from near and far were gathering. The range was too dry to support both wild horses and beef cattle. One drought summer had succeeded another, and grass conditions had grown increasingly serious. The horses had to go. I knew that very well, although I was sick at heart about them. All my life in that region I had seen them racing down the ridges against the sky, and watching them, I knew what it meant to be free. Now their hides would go for leather, their hooves for glue, their muscles for dog food. And my father was going to do it.

I voiced every argument I could think of as we drove. Why not drive the wild horses to Idaho or down into Wyoming or onto the sheep range that lay to the north?

"The day of the wild horse is past, son," my father said crisply. In my head I knew he was right.

The road lay across prairie and hills, eighty miles to the point where we turned off after it crossed Pumpkin Creek. We drove under Sam's high crossbar gate and over the cattle guard and followed the ranch road for almost a mile until we came to the crest of a hill and looking south we saw all the buildings of Sam Tolliver's ranch spread out below us: the low, white ranch house, the log bunkhouse and the carbide light house and the pump house and the white icehouse, a pond for watering horses, the great hay and tack barn, a cow shed, the horse barn roofed by sod, and the pole corrals. Rising from the corrals was a great cloud of yellow dust and shouts and whinnies and the drum of hooves.

We left the car under a cottonwood, rolled up the windows to keep out the dust and flies, and walked toward the corrals into the midst of the biggest wild horse roundup in that part of Montana.

The sorting corrals, the branding corrals, the enclosures to vaccinate and dehorn, all of them surged with wild horses. There were cowboys from all over in and out and on the fences, swinging their ropes to get the horses to run in the right direction past the buyers. Men from horsemeat plants as far away as the Twin Cities leaned on the top rail and watched with shrewd, flickering horse-trader eyes. The brand inspectors observed and waited.

Immediately my father turned here and there, shaking hands, preparing to do business. He lifted his hand in greeting. "There's Tom Driscoll." I was quick to look, because Tom Driscoll was the most respected cowman in those parts.

At that moment he stood alone in the great corral, watching the activity beyond the gate. He was a big man, and in his leather chaps and high-heeled boots he looked even bigger. More than size, he had a presence which drew your eye. He waited, both alert and at ease, his weight on one foot, his arms hanging, and looking at him, I was struck with one thought: he really knows what he's doing! He acknowledged my father with a raised gloved hand.

The next moment he was joined by Seth McCollum whom I had seen in the stockyards in town. He was rumored to be seventy, maybe eighty years old, so old that he had done everything the region had to offer: hunted buffalo, rustled cattle, hired out as a vigilante, married a squaw once, and run his own cattle. He was tall and thin and still erect, and he wore a hat stiff-crowned and flat-brimmed in a style no longer worn on the range. By age and appearance and reputation he stood out from all the others. There was a grandeur about him.

He turned his back on the horsemeat buyers. When my father spoke to him, he seemed not to hear. My loyalties split and ripped me in two.

We moved along the corral fence, and a man came toward us, holding out his hand and pushing back his hat. This was Sam Tolliver. We exchanged greetings, and Sam put his arm around my shoulders. "How's the new horse wrangler?" I couldn't help grinning. "Come along with me and get into this business."

Sam moved down the fence, and I followed. Where there was room, he put a foot up on the bottom rail and leaned on the rail shoulder-high and looked between the bars. I did the same, and together we watched for a few minutes without speaking.

Sam was in his early fifties, and the hair which showed under his hat was iron gray. He stood nearly six feet tall and was strong and fit but for a slight bulge over his belt. His eyes were a bleached blue, Western prairie eyes accustomed to picking out objects miles away which can only be identified by shape and movement.

In the dust and noise and hooting and hollering a bunch of horses swept close by me.

"Aren't they beautiful?" Sam said. "It's a shame, Goddam, but it's a shame. Look at that little sorrel maverick. Any other time he'd be worth plenty."

Seth McCollum crossed the corral, and when he came close, you could see that he was a very old man. In spite of his height and erectness the flesh had shrunk away from his bones and his hands were like knotted sticks wrapped in brown spotted paper. Sam said, "You know Billy Catlett, Charley's boy?" Seth looked at me as if he saw me from some enormous distance and noted my contours and my brand, but if he said anything, I couldn't detect it. To him I guessed I was the son of a horsemeat buyer.

"Is Fonse ready?" Sam said, and Seth replied, "All ready." "See you later, Billy," Sam said and climbed over the fence into the great corral.

The herd of horses was being held down at one end by Tom Driscoll and three cowboys, and when Sam and Seth crossed the pen, Sam yelled, "Let 'em go!" They let a few loose and, hooting and hollering, chased them along the fence toward Seth and Sam. As they thundered by, Seth read and called out the brands loud and clear. Around the top rail the ranchers and cowboys and ranchers' reps — representatives — stood waiting, and when his brand was called out, a man yelled, "Mine!" and his name, and the bookkeeper, who sat on the top rail, marked it carefully down.

When the horses were identified and claimed, Sam yelled, "Open up," and the hand working the gate swung it outward, protecting himself by staying on the far side. At that moment the little sorrel maverick broke away from the unclaimed and raced through the open gate.

18

"Stop him!" Sam yelled, but he kicked viciously, his hooves sounding against the gate planks, and no one could stop him. "We'll get him later."

Then the buying for the slaughterhouses began. I moved down the fence, listening to the bidding. I heard my father's voice, saw him make the buying sign as I passed behind the buyers to the next corral.

Cowboys were moving among the claimed horses, cussing spectacularly while they roped and sorted their own. The little maverick hid in the center of the bunch.

"Get that son of a bitch out of here," one big red-faced cowboy yelled. "He's stirrin' 'em up," I opened the corral gate, and they hustled the little horse through.

Now he ran in a corral which was for the moment empty. I stood inside and watched him. He was as pretty a horse as I had ever seen. His sorrel hide was nicked and scarred from bites and fights and barbed wire, and his sorrel mane was long and tangled, and his broomtail a knot of burrs. Still he was beautiful. His head flung up and his eye glinting, he had the spirit and intelligence to outwit his captors. If I had the nerve, I could help him. I crossed the corral to the next gate.

"Hey, you! You pistol!"

I froze. Pistol was another name for a boy. Whoever it was meant me. I turned slowly.

Tom Driscoll came straight for me. He wore heavy leather chaps with his initials and brand cut in the sides, and his spur rowels rang with every step. He was covered with dust, and in his armpits were dark rings of sweat and white lines where sweat had dried between jobs. He looked even bigger than he had earlier.

"What're you doin', pistol?"

I swallowed. "I wasn't going to let him out free."

Tom looked at me curiously.

"I just hated to see him sold for horsemeat, once he got away on his own, I mean, by himself . . ."

Tom took out his tobacco sack and papers and rolled and licked a twisted cigarette. "He's one of the best of the bunch," he said.

"I can buy him. I don't have any money with me, but . . ."

"He won't go for horsemeat. He'll make somebody a good ridin' horse." Exhaling. "His price will be a lot more than the doggers."

Disappointment sank through me, surprising me. I wanted that horse.

"The mavericks belong to Sam. They were on his land. Maybe when this's done with, if the horse's still here, you can make a deal with Sam." With one gloved hand he shot open the plank which secured the gate. "Run him into the little stall behind the barn. Maybe nobody'll see him there." He passed through the gate and was gone.

From one corral to the next I drove the little horse. Where he tried to disappear among his kind, other cowboys helped me. The maverick raced ahead of me, turning where he could, finally into the small enclosure in the barn's shadow. From the far side he watched me. I locked the gate and hurried away.

I took a conspicuous place along the main corral. Tom Driscoll was there with his back toward me. His dirty black hat, his shoulders high and wide as if they carried his weight, the seat of his Levi's sticking out above his leather chaps, these were all I could see of him. He and Sam and Seth ran the whole show.

Herd after herd passed through the corral. Many of the horses had brands and were claimed. The rest were mavericks, unbranded and wild, and they were the doggers. If no one bought them, the ones which might make good working horses, they were fated for the glue pots. These my father looked over with the buyers from the Twin Cities. All that beautiful wildness which ate the range needed for cattle was going, going, gone.

After a decent interval I wandered away, ducked through the barn and came out by the one-horse corral. The sorrel maverick was still there. I sat on the top rail and watched him. If I was a cowboy and had a string, he would be my favorite. I would call him — maybe Pumpkin. Sorrels were often called that, and here on Pumpkin Creek that wouldn't be too bad. Still I wanted a special name. The way the sun rippled across his rough coat made me think of Going-Down-the-Sun, the name of a great Blackfoot chief. Sundown would be shorter. Only there was something sad about it. He was one of the last of the wild horses, in the sundown of their days, so I'd give him another name, not Sundown, but Sundance, for his rippling, pumpkin-colored coat and the glinting spirit in his wild eye. I saw myself riding Sundance to glory in the corral and alone across the prairie as I searched my limitless imaginary lands for stray cattle.

About midday a gong summoned everybody from the corrals to the trestle tables set up under the cottonwoods near the house. Each of us took a tin plate and went up and down the tables, helping ourselves — fried chicken and home-canned beef in gravy and green beans and cold tomatoes and dunes of mashed potatoes and gigantic pans of baked beans and mixing bowls of sliced

cucumbers and onions in vinegar and stacks of white
bread, chocolate cake and five kinds of pie, a crock of
lemonade and a big white enamel pot of coffee.

With a heaping plateful I followed my father and
Sam where they moved under the trees and squatted on
their haunches to eat and talk, and I listened and
mopped my plate. After a while Tom Driscoll joined us,
balancing his plate on the leather chaps over one knee,
and he grinned at me and blinked both eyes and said,
"How'd it go, Pistol?" And I grinned and said, "Okay."

The talk was about weather and the prolonged dry
spell. "It's lasting too long," Sam said. "Now when the
rain comes, the lightning storms will send up the prairie
like a match. It doesn't look good."

"The blue joint grass's pretty fair along the crick
bottom," Tom said. "Now the horses are out of it, there
should be a crop."

"Hope so," Sam said. "I'd hate to think this horse
roundup was for nothing."

After dinner I watched Tom Driscoll work the herds,
and I watched the buyers and ranchers and old Seth
McCollum and the reps from more distant places up the
Mizpah, from Lame Deer and Broadus, who were on the
lookout for lost horses.

I leaned against the rail with Sam when he stopped to
light a cigarette. He smoked tailor-mades. After a long
whiff of smoke he said, "We'll have to get you a horse,
Billy. Have you seen one around here you like pretty
well?"

My heart thumped like a tom-tom, and my throat
went dry. I forced a huge breath and said, "I kind of
like the little sorrel maverick. When he got loose from

the bunch, I ran him into the stall behind the barn. He's still there."

Sam nodded and blew smoke. "That's a nice horse. I'll have Tom break him for you. He'll be your horse while you're out here."

That was the greatest and most glorious day of my life. Besides being born, which must be the most important because otherwise nothing can happen to you, it was the best day I had ever lived.

It was June 1930.

Riding Circle

3

The cowboys drove knots of horses out the road. Cars loaded up and were driven away. The activity in the corrals subsided as the yellow dust settled again to earth.

By the time my father helped me with my duffle and saddle and shook my hand, I trembled with nervousness. It wasn't too late to jump in the car with him. A minute later it was too late. With a dry mouth, wet palms and a banging heart, I shouldered my duffle and dragged my saddle toward Sam's ranch house.

On one side of the open porch stood a big brown-stained wood icebox with double doors and a pan under it to catch the melting ice. Next to it was the cream separator covered with a faded sheet blanket. On the other side of the door was a washstand with an enamel basin, a bucket and dipper underneath and a mottled mirror and wooden pegs for hats up above. The door opened into an enormous kitchen violently hot from the wood cookstove and already steaming with supper. A

24

sturdy woman in a housedress and apron worked at the stove, and a girl, maybe out of high school, was laying the long table, covered with red-printed oilcloth, which filled the middle of the kitchen.

"Mrs. Gallagher, this is Billy Catlett," Sam said, "and, Billy, this is Lacey Barnett from over to Lame Deer. She's helping out this summer." I said, "Howdy," and Lacey smiled a little over her shoulder, and Mrs. Gallagher said with good nature, "I'll need wood tomorrow, Billy."

The kitchen opened into a living room kept dim against the heat of the day. It didn't look used much. The fireplace was dark and vacant, and a faint smell of dust rose from the cushioned chairs. Off that room were three bedrooms, Sam's, the one shared by Mrs. Gallagher and Lacey, and a third which was really a lean-to attached to the house with a door knocked through the wall. It was small and made of rough lumber hastily wallpapered with lilacs, and the ceiling beams had been painted white and the bed was homemade, just four squares with a mattress on top and a white cover. I took to it right off.

There was not time for me to stow my gear in the brown-stained bureau before I heard the screen slamming and creaking, and I knew the hands were gathering for the evening meal. I reached the kitchen just as Tom Driscoll came in and we grinned and he said, "Howdy, Pistol." Behind him was old Seth McCollum with his eyes that looked at me and didn't seem to see me; then a lanky drifter named Texas Diller; the big red-headed puncher called, naturally, Red; Fonse, a small and wiry man, the bookkeeper from the roundup; and last of all came a fellow named Roscoe, carrying the milk pails. Roscoe noticed me immediately and began asking little questions like "Where'd you work before this?" and I answered as politely as the smallest amount of information could make it. I knew where a cowboy stood who milked the cows: on the bottom.

We ranged around the long table with Sam in the armchair at the head and me taking a place two chairs away across from Tom Driscoll. All the places were filled but one. It was the tradition on ranches in those days to set an extra place for any passing friend or stranger. Any cowboy riding across country knew that the place where he found himself at nightfall had set an extra plate, and that he was welcome to stop, take a hand with the chores, share the evening meal and the bunkhouse and drift on in the morning.

"Oh, my, how my tooth does hurt," Texas Diller said, amusing everybody just by the way he said it. "I shoulda gone to town, I just knew I shoulda."

"You would have," Red said, "if you wasn't scared to death of the tooth jerker."

"I know it, I know it," Texas drawled, "the sight of that drill just sets me to buckin' something fierce."

"I don't know when I'm going in," Sam said, "but if it hurts you too bad, I'll take a day off."

"No, no," Texas said, "I don't want to put you out, Sam. I'll just suffer along."

After the laughter, they began to discuss the next day's work. The cattle had not been rounded up yet. The big wild horse drive had put off the usual early summer work, the June roundup and branding and counting of new calves and winter losses.

"Riding circle tomorrow, boys," Sam said.

"What's this here Pistol goin' to do for us that we

can't do for ourselves?" Red said. My nervousness almost mounted to a shudder again.

"I've hired Pistol on as horse wrangler."

"We don't have no real gentle horses for a kid to ride," Fonse said. Not one of them looked at me.

"Tom will take him out the first few days and show him the ropes."

"I don't see Driscoll as no kind of teacher," Red said. "That kid last year never did learn nothin'. Driscoll just babied him along when he needed a boot in the rear. Now I can learn Pistol here about all he needs to know so's he won't forget it in maybe two days."

"We don't have no more time to spare," Texas said.

"I sure hope Pistol can ride good," Fonse said, and Texas murmured, "Sure do, Pistol." Now Seth McCollum looked at me with distant interest.

Apprehension chilled me. They took up Tom's nickname for me and gave it a sardonic edge, emphasizing its substitute for "boy" rather than for Billy. They put a lump of fear in my stomach that rose and fell. Tom was grinning at me as he bent over his coffee.

"See you at the corral first thing," Tom said.

"I'll be there." If both my legs were broken in nineteen places, I knew I'd make it.

The morning lay lightly across the pine hills when I wakened. The first horizontal shafts of sun were no warmer than the night of a few minutes before. I kept my jumper jacket buttoned walking down the road to the corrals. Everything rested in stillness. I thought I was alone in the tack barn when Tom came through the doorway, carrying his saddle, a tiny dead cigarette crimped in his lips. He nodded to me and smiled. I brought out my saddle and Tom bridled and led out two horses. "Try this one, Pistol," he said. Knowing he was watching me as he worked, I moved up to the strange horse, took the reins, patted him, waited, threw on the blanket and waited, swung up the saddle and, moving slowly, gathered in the cinch and pulled it tight. Taking the inside rein up tight, and a fistful of mane in one hand, I turned the stirrup forward, grasped the horn and swung on. The horse was off and prancing before I sat well down, and Tom was waiting, already in the saddle, watching. He said nothing, only smiled a little with his lips closed on the dead cigarette and I guessed my horsemanship passed for the moment, and we set out at a high trot toward the north pasture where the horses were turned out for the night.

As the sun touched my cheekbone, as the damp grasses grew warm and fragrant and their shadows shortened, a little wind stirred the surface and a pine wren chippered lost to sight in the needled branches. We circled north and east, keeping to a high ridge, and Tom said, "Look for that big black Sam rides. The rest will be right near him. That little maverick is out here, too." He looked for sign, hoofprints, manure, movement in the distant hillsides and unusually deep shadow in the washes. "There he is," he said. I followed, not saying that I saw nothing, searching everywhere for what he had seen until there in the long shadow half a mile down the coulee I saw the contours of the big black. We swept down the wash, chasing out the others before us. The big black horse led at a gallop, and Tom lit out at full run and turned him the way he wanted him to go, the others following, turning this way and that but always being driven toward the open gates leading to the corrals. I didn't see the sorrel maverick that day.

The corrals were stirring as we drove the horses in. As soon as I closed the pole gate, Red swung his rope, and it whistled over the head of a wiry bay that reared and snorted. "Come on, you Roman-nosed son of a bitch," Red growled, "don't give me no trouble." Seth Mc-Collum moved slowly toward his horse until he could rope him easily and talk to him and lead him to the fence. When Fonse threw his rope into the bunch, he missed and sent them stampeding around the fence. The cowboys leapt out of the way, yelling, "Jesus Christ," and vaulting the fence like acrobats. Red's horse started bucking with Red yelling, "Don't try nothing fancy with me," and pulling the horse's head back almost even with the saddle horn.

Going up to the main house for breakfast, we met Texas Diller limping down the road. "What's the matter?" Tom asked. "Oh, my, oh, my, my boot shrunk in the night," Texas said. "Your tooth still hurtin'?" "I don't know yet, soon as my foot eases up, I can tell you."

Sam led out of the corral with the riders bunched a little behind him. The sun rose higher, already hot. Now there was rising dust and growing heat, wind and dryness. We rode quickly through two gates into a higher area of the pine hills. As we moved along, not stopping, every so often Sam assigned two riders to a certain territory, and they dropped out of the ranks, disappearing over the brow of a hill or growing smaller as they scrambled down a stony draw. Toward mid-morning he said, "Tom, you take Pistol here and cover that section around Hopper's Well." Immediately we left the line and set off across country to the area meant for us.

By riding circle the grazing land of a ranch could be scoured for all the cows and calves and last year's steers, its own or anyone else's, that had wandered onto its range. The calves could be counted, the sick ones doctored, the losses assessed, the mavericks branded.

As we rode, I studied Tom and everything about him. How he wore his hat, how he tied his jumper jacket to the back of his saddle, how he rode, how he took the jounce of his horse on the balls of his feet, in the knees and in the shoulders, how he stood in the stirrups with the reins held almost over the horse's ears when he wanted a fast trot. To me he was the ideal cowman, a big man with huge shoulders and narrow hips. His Levi's fit him tight, and his blue denim work shirt was too tight across the chest. He had a large, round head and a broad face, open and freckled, that would have been round, too, if it hadn't been so lean and hard, and a big, wonderful grin. He was a superb horseman, and that day he rode a small, sinewy animal so out of proportion that the stirrups dangled below his belly. After watching awhile I could see why he picked that little horse. It was fast and quick and responsive and so well trained as a cow horse that it knew as well as Tom what to do.

Over the crest of a hill half a dozen cows with calves nibbled the tall grass; the cows raised their heavy heads to regard us. The calves bawled when we rode close and whooped it up to get them started. The cows trotted away and stopped, looking back. When they saw we meant business, they fell into line and moved ahead.

Tom sent me off first in one direction, then another, to sweep a hillside or a hidden coulee. I followed the pattern that Tom used, but it wasn't so easy as Tom made it look. A mean old cow would light out around me, and it was half an hour before I could turn it back and get the bunch together again and going in the right direction. Then, when I caught up to Tom, he had added twice as many in the time I took to circle three or four. When five yearling steers took off in five different directions, I wondered if I'd ever learn. When I brought a bunch in to the main herd and saw Tom, I knew that if I kept on watching him, I would learn everything I needed to know.

Tom clamped one little dead twisted cigarette after another between his lips as we worked. He didn't swear; he didn't say anything. Even when I made a mistake and messed up a whole strategy, he didn't say a word. We just started all over again, from the beginning. We had finally brought the bunch into line, when an ornery little black steer broke loose and hightailed it over the next hill.

"Go get him, Pistol," Tom said. "I'll meet you down the way." Standing in my stirrups and holding the reins high above the horse's ears, as I had seen Tom do, I raced after the steer. Just over the crest of the hill I lost him. I rode up and down, searching every direction. There he was, down below, standing very still in the black shadow of a pine. I circled around him to drive him from the other side. He broke past me, and we were off again in the wrong direction. I caught up with him, swinging my rope and hitting him with it to turn him, and he turned. I turned. He pivoted and raced away. I turned again and ran after him, hitting him and turning him. This time we went round and round in a circle. I ran through every sulfurous noun and adjective in my vocabulary, finding none of them sufficient. That's why Tom didn't swear; it didn't help any. The cursed, lunkheaded steer knew he had me. He led me up and down the grassy draw between two hills; he spun me round and round until he could gallop over the next hill and hide among the rocks. Sweat poured down my spine and chest. My hat was soaked around the band, making it uncomfortably tight and sticky. "I'll kill you," I whispered, "wait till I get you, just wait, just wait."

An hour went by. I could not turn that steer. I could not drive him where I needed him to go. I stopped and rested, trying to figure out something, under a pine tree. He stopped two trees away and waited, watching me. I tried to outwait him, thinking that he would start grazing after a while, but not that knuckleheaded beast. He didn't take his eyes off me. I tried riding away. It didn't fool him. I tried riding over the hill, circling back, and coming up behind him. He was looking my way. Then I began chasing him again, up and down, round and round, cussing helplessly, hitting him with the rope, and finally streaming with the sweat down my face were tears of anger and frustration. I wiped them, tears, dirt, and sweat, on my sleeve and still they streamed down.

It seemed like all day, maybe a week, a month that I had chased that little black steer when I saw Tom appear on the brow of the hill and ride quickly, taking a diagonal path, down the rocky slope. As he came near me, he glanced across my face, although I was past caring, and as he rode by me, he said, "Pistol, there is only one way to handle a critter like that." Under a pine he swung off his horse and picked up a dead branch thick as my arm, swung into the saddle again, and rode after that bedeviled lunkheaded black steer.

When he came abreast of him, Tom lifted the branch and brought it down on the steer's head right between his eyes. The steer staggered in his tracks. Tom turned and shooed it in front of him. When they reached me, I fell in beside Tom and he handed me the branch. "Sometimes you got to clobber 'em," he said.

As we brought them along the road toward the main herd, we passed a cool green, marshy area where a spring broke through the surface crust. There Tom dismounted, and we drank, lying flat on the cool ground. Tom took off his hat and splashed his face, and I followed, rubbing to get rid of the tear streaks through the dust.

I first saw the plume of smoke ahead, rising above the hill and drifting away on the wind, and the bellering of the small herd Tom and I drove blended with the bellering and mooing of the big herd held unseen behind the hill. Whooping and hollering, swinging my rope, I rode around the flank of the bunch to turn them into the draw, toward the main herd, and as I came up into the wind, the stench hit me, the nose-lacerating stink of burning hair. The branding had already begun.

Below me in a broad buff-colored meadow in a ring of pine-spotted buff-colored stony hills lay the main herd gathered that day and held in the open without restraining ropes or pole corrals by horses and riders standing, sitting, almost idly, around the edge. The branding fire burned low and hot, and the great black irons wrought into flying W's, lazy K's, rocking R's, bar circle A and circle A bar lay half in, half out of the blue-white coals. The branding fire marked the center of that day's circle.

Suddenly I saw Red turn his horse, cut a calf from the herd, catch its heels with his rope and bring it to earth. Before it scrambled to its feet again, Red's horse dragged it to the fire.

Around the fire men I hadn't seen before now gathered. Some had shown up looking for strays. Terence Mitchell, the remittance man who ranched on the other side of Sam's place, stood by. Outside of his cinnamon walrus moustache, he looked more like a cowboy than a cowboy. His clothes were dirtier and more worn, and not a bit of decoration glorified his boots. I had always heard he was a black sheep, the son of an English lord who shipped him off to America and sent him money, a remittance, to stay away. Maybe it was true. Nobody knew really. Very few people had ever been to the Mitchell ranch where, it was another rumor, the women wore long dresses to dinner.

The riders spread out and made room for our herd to join, disappear among the others. Saying, "You hold 'em there, Pistol," Tom rode off to the fire and I sat my horse on the edge of the herd, feeling suddenly weary as the idleness set in, my bottom and the inside of my thighs aching from hours in the saddle. I wanted to get down and walk around a little, but I knew better. That would be the moment for some kind of stampede, and I wouldn't be ready to hold my side or, worse, I'd get trampled. I leaned my weight first on one stirrup, then the other, trying to stretch and ease the aching muscles.

Not far away Texas Diller sat his horse with one knee hooked over the saddle horn, talking to Seth McCollum, and gradually I moved within listening distance to hear

Texas drawling, "You're just so durn old you don't hurt anymore," and Seth McCollum reply, "I'm too old to buy my boots smaller'n my feet."

I really took a shine to Seth's hat. There wasn't another like it. From a long way off it told what the man who wore it was, an old-timer, a survivor in a rugged land. I edged nearer.

"They aren't smaller'n my feet," Texas said, "it's just that overnight they kinduv shrink up on me."

"You should sleep in 'em," Seth McCollum said.

"Now there's a mighty good idea," Texas said. "Maybe I couldn't sleep, but I wouldn't have no trouble gettin' 'em on in the mornin'."

To my pleasure Seth McCollum's faded blue eyes gathered focus on me. He noticed me in the flesh for the first time. He spoke to me. "Pistol, you going to chase these steers ass backwards?"

My face went hot and red. I had moved closer and closer, never noticing that now I held my horse with his rear to the herd. I began to stammer when I heard Tom yell, "Hey, Pistol, come take a hand here," and I turned my horse toward the fire.

Dragging a calf on his long rope behind him, Tom rode into the branding range, and when he stopped, his horse held the rope taut while Fonse flanked the calf.

"Get the hind feet there, Pistol," he yelled at me, and I grabbed the two hind legs. The calf was incredibly strong, and I had to hook one hock under the heel and instep of my boot to hold him. "For Chrissake, hold him," Fonse snapped, and I held for dear life. The calf bellered and heaved as Fonse twisted his head to keep him thrown on the ground, and swiftly and deftly Terence Mitchell notched the ears, and Sam approached with the white-hot iron gripped in his gloved hands. "Hold him, Pistol, hold him," Fonse yelled, and I strained to hold the hind legs. If they flew out of my hands, Fonse would be kicked by the razor clefts in the hooves, the hot iron might hit one of us, but the calf was stronger than I was. I exerted every muscle I had to the limit as the white iron came down on the hide and the smoke and the lacerating stench and sizzle rose from the little calf's hip and his eye bulged and rolled white and his rear end squirted brown, putrid excrement down the legs. Sam lifted the brand with the hair gone and the hide burned brown and stepped back, and a rep called Fickinger leaned forward with his many years sharpened pocketknife extended and slit the testicles with the calf making another heave and bawling and the brown eye rolling out of sight, and Fickinger reached inside and pulled out the sacs and cut them away from the tubes and stepped back to give Sam room to daub the cut with pine tar and Fickinger held up the sacs and said, "I'll save them for ya, Pistol. You can cook 'em later. That'll make a man of you." Fonse grinned at me, loosening the rope, and then hollered, "Let 'im go!" and I let go and jumped back and the little calf scrambled to his feet and raced away to the herd bellering for his mother, and I marveled.

I wrestled the hind legs of calf after calf until I knew I couldn't do it again and then wrestled some more. Texas took my place and I rode back to the herd dirtier than I had ever been in my life and more exhausted, my shirt torn where a hoof had broken away from me for a second, the tail out. I sat my horse on the hillside on the edge of the herd where I could see all of the wide meadow between the hills, the herd encircled by riders, their horses facing the cattle, poised and alert, knowing as much as the men, more, some of them, and, a distance away, the branding fire and the furious activity there, and the smoke and the stench drifting away into the hot sky over the buff-colored meadow.

All afternoon the ropers brought the new calves from the herd and wrestled them down while they were branded and castrated and had their ears notched so that in the deep drifts of winter when the curly coats hid the brand and nothing much showed but heads and backs, a calf or a cow could be identified.

When all the strays were identified and all the calves branded, the herd was released, and we returned to the ranch for supper and the night. I was tired beyond feeling, hungry beyond knowing, and sitting on the edge of my bed, pulling off one boot, I thought, it was terrible, pulling off the other boot, it was brutal, unbuttoning my shirt, it was the way it was, undoing the rivet buttons on my fly, the way it had to be, and I lay down and slept.

For several days we rode circle from the main ranch, until those sections had been well combed for new calves and mavericks. Gradually I was not so worn-out by night, but I was always gnawing with hunger. After a few mornings Tom left me to wrangle the horses alone. It took longer, and sometimes I saw the little sorrel horse watching me from a ridge, and I tried to drive him in, an offense he didn't permit. When I brought the bunch into the corral, Fonse said, "I thought we lost you this time, Pistol."

"I worked this ranch once," Texas said, "where they had this big dog, and he was the smartest horse wrangler I ever did see."

Then Red started. He kept on doing what he was doing, watching me and giving me a running commentary on my mistakes. Then everything went wrong. I had an uneasy truce with the wrangling horse, anyway, and he acted up. Red criticized freely. And when they had me sore and sweating, they quit. That way they let me know I was living.

Tom said nothing, saddling up, grinning a little with the little dead pinched cigarette between his lips and looking humorously at me. Tom never ridiculed me. He never cussed me out the way Red did. He didn't say much of anything, but he let me know that I could make it and I would.

Every day Sam assigned me to a rider. Usually it was Tom. I ground my teeth when I had to go with Red. He was almost as good a hand as Tom, which I had to respect, but I didn't have to like him. Every once in a while I had a chance to ride with Seth. He didn't criticize me. He didn't take notice. With sixty years between us I guess he figured there wasn't much to say. One noon as we rode through the north pasture, he raised his twiglike finger and pointed and said, "Buffalo trail. It's nearly gone now."

At first I saw nothing, and then under the stones and grass I detected a faint worn, depressed path.

"They came this way," he said, "heading for water. We waited for them down below."

"Was the grass high then, up to a horse's belly?"

The old head under the flat-brimmed hat nodded. "Longhorns killed the grass. They came and covered this prairie like water." He said no more.

When the day's work was over and supper eaten, we settled down on the edge of the porch. Texas leaned against a post and Tom rolled another cigarette and Fonse leafed through a cowboy outfitter's catalog and tried to touch Sam for his pay in advance so that he could order a pair of boots decorated from top to ankle with magnificent yellow butterflies.

"They'll just pinch your feet," Texas said.

"You've borrowed your pay up to January now," Sam said.

"Fonse got a real hanker for those butterflies." Tom grinned. "If you see yourself in butterfly boots, it's sure hard to do without 'em."

Right then Red rode his horse up the road and out of sight, never looking our way. Everybody smoked and watched him in silence. Fonse said, "The Widow Garrison must be back."

Each night I hoped and waited for Seth McCollum to spin a yarn, a tale of the old days when the grass had swept the horses' bellies and the longhorns had come up from Texas, when the Indians were hostiles and the vigilantes had ridden, but Seth McCollum told no tales at all. The punchers kidded him about his silence, saying, "You can't go to jail for nothin' that happened so long ago," and, "The judge'd be merciful, Seth, account of your age. You're older'n he is." Seth smiled and looked them over with his bloodshot, watery eyes and kept his silence.

When the close-in areas had been worked, we set out for the high grazing land in the national forest. From somewhere appeared a man called Greasy Granger whom Sam had hired as cook for the days we'd be out. The chuck wagon was hauled in and loaded with supplies and bedrolls of soogans, homemade quilts, and canvas. It took four men cussing in unison to heave the

39

old iron cookstove onto the back and strap it in place with the chuck box behind it. That day we rode for the high country farther into the pine hills than I had been before.

Each day we rode circle over a certain area, driving the herd to a central point where the branding was done, and each night we made camp. One night we threw our bedrolls in an open meadow. Another night the outpost camp had a house and a corral and a dug well. Riders showed up from other outfits. Allie Bassett from the Bassett brothers' place appeared with his cowboys, and Dominic Arlo, who was the son of a Basque sheepherder turned cattleman, rode in with his pack horse and a saddle string. On the government land there were no fences to keep one man's stock separated from another's, and a rancher had to seek out his strays or send his rep, because the mavericks were finder's keepers.

On the fourth day out the crowd had grown to the point where Greasy Granger said he was running out of meat. Sam took his .30-30 from the sheath under his stirrup leather; Red separated a yearling from the bunch we had just driven in and Sam shot it on the spot. Two of them working together tied the rope to the hind feet and pulled the carcass up to a pine branch. They gripped their skinning knives and cut off the hide, disemboweling as they went. The carcass had just begun to stiffen when they cut it into quarters, sliced off steaks and threw them into the frying pans waiting over the branding fires. I had a little trouble appreciating my slice, but I ate it.

That night Texas Diller moaned and groaned in his bedroll, waking everybody up. "Now which is it," Red said, "your foot or your head? Cause whichever it is I'm going to chop it off."

"Now that's kinduv rough talk when a fellow's sufferin'," Texas said. "It's my tooth again, I knew I shouldn'tuv chewed with it."

Stumbling to the chuck wagon, Greasy Granger gave him some cloves to suck, muttering, "And keep your mouth shut while you're doing it."

So went the days and nights when I first went to Sam's place. Wrangling alone in the early morning, riding circle with the men over vast reaches of grass and rock and pine hill, filling myself to overstuffed twice a day at Greasy Granger's hot black stove, toting water for the reservoir tank on one end of it and wood to stoke it, listening to the cowboy talk at night around the fire and trying so hard not to laugh out loud that my whole body ached, crawling between my soogans to sleep as inert as the big branch Tom used to turn that contrary little black steer. To me it was a perfect world, the perfect life.

Breaking The
Little Maverick

4

One evening soon after we were back in the main ranch, Tom said to me, rolling his after-dinner cigarette, "I'll go out with you in the mornin', Pistol, and we'll see if we can bring in that little maverick. We'd better start to gentle him."

I pressed my teeth together to contain the wash of excitement that went over me, and I said, "Gee, that'll be great, Tom."

The range had grown drier and drier, and that morning no dew moistened the brown grass. Long early shadows stretched across the hard prairie hills turning clumps of sagebrush into trees on the ground, the fence posts into telephone poles, a grasshopper huddled on top of one into a creature. As he waited for the warming sun I flicked him with the end of the reins and he dropped in an arc into the grass. I felt a twang of remorse and muttered, "Everybody has to get up, buddy."

Tom knew almost by instinct where the herd lay, and he seemed to have a good idea where the little maverick might hide himself, because we sighted him without much difficulty in the deep shadow between boulders and a knot of pine. Driving him out was another matter. We circled and came up behind him, sending him galloping ahead, his sorrel mane and tail floating on the wind, in the direction of the corrals. Shortly he caught on to this and tried to race between us, but Tom on his swift cutting pony turned him back. Next, he tried to break out of Tom's side, and again Tom's skill and the swiftness and sureness of his horse cut off the escape. The little horse was no dummy. After a few tries he discovered that I wasn't either as quick or as clever as Tom, and he attempted all his escapes past me. Slowly, painfully, working until I was wringing wet, we cut back and forth until we drove the little horse through the gate and into the lane leading to the corrals. Once he was alone in the snubbing corral, we left him until after breakfast.

"Pistol," Tom said as we leaned together on the pole fence, watching him, "I think we can gentle this horse without being too rough on him. You'll get a better horse that way. He won't have no meanness to remember." He let himself down into the corral. "But he's in for a rude jolt at the start."

With the loop of his rope half concealed at his side Tom approached the horse as he waited with one bulging eye watching. With the speed of light the rope flew out and settled over his neck. The little horse broke

43

away; Tom dug in his heels, leaning backwards, and slid through the dust after the horse. I crawled between the fence poles, took up the end of the rope, and dug in behind Tom. Now the little horse gave a little slack and then a burst of speed. When he hit the end of the rope, we held him and he snapped around like a whip. Standing still, staring at us, snorting and gasping, his wild thoughts seemed easy to me to read.

"Now that's just a rope, see," Tom was crooning, as he worked hand over hand toward the little horse. "It's not so bad." Tom patted the quivering neck. "You'll get so you like it," and he grinned a little, sardonically. "Bring the hackamore, Pistol." He stroked the neck gently and firmly. "You're a very pretty animal," he said, "and I think you've got some sense." Tom tried to stroke the ears where the hackamore had to pass, holding the rope near the snuffling snout, and then swiftly and deftly settling the hackamore in place. "Now-now-now," he sang, "you don't want to act up. That'll just rile us both."

Then Tom removed his own rope and let the little horse race away, wearing the hackamore. "Come on, Pistol," he said. "We'll just leave him like that and work with him a little more this afternoon."

The little maverick learned quickly about the long rope. After being caught two or three times and being snapped like a whip when he raced to the end of his tether, he gave up that act entirely and waited for his next opening.

"This way it'll take till hell freezes over to break that horse," Red said. "You're goin' to be all summer at it."

"Maybe," Tom said.

"You snub a horse in the corral and he'll learn in two minutes what you're goin' to take a week to learn him," Red said. I looked from Red to Tom.

"That doesn't mean he learns it right," Tom said.

The ranch work was behind, I knew that. Maybe I ought to speak up.

Red's voice took on a certain edge. "You can't protect a kid from a bucker. He's goin' to meet up with one someday."

Startled, I looked at Tom and saw his jaw clench and his eyes glitter, and he waited quite a while before he replied, "What you can ride don't make a man of you. How you ride him makes the difference."

Now we had reached the house and Tom doused his head in the washbasin beside the door and put an end to the conversation.

After the day's work was done, Tom said, "Come on, Pistol, we'll see what that little maverick's been doin'."

In the corral, his sorrel red darkened with sweat, Sundance waited, and when he saw us appear above the top rail of the high pole fence, he ran off, wildly, nickering for rescue in one long bugling cry.

"He's got a lot of spirit, Pistol," Tom said. "We don't want to break it, just tame it some and use it."

That night we staked him to a great fallen tree outside of the corrals, because, Tom said, he wasn't going to live his life in an enclosure. Tom used not the hard twisted hemp of the usual rope but a soft, strong kind that would not burn, and he held Sundance not with a slipknot at the neck but a secure knot which would hold him without choking his wind. As soon as we let him go, he ran to the end of his tether and snapped around. His eyes bulging, his flanks heaving, he stared at the rope and at us, his captors. Then he flung up his chiseled head and whinnied again, such a long wild nicker that the muscles along his ribs showed as he expended the air. My heart thumped wildly. "We'll just leave him there the night," Tom said, and he turned away, drawing me with him and away from the wild desire to let him go that came over me.

My sleep was restless that night, and when I woke and lay on my back staring at the dim ceiling, I heard that wild, lonely nicker out on the prairie and the timid answers from two or three horses in the corrals. Lying there, listening, I knew I wanted him more than I wanted to release him, and the choice was mine, not his.

A number of days passed before Sundance came to accept the rope with only a little suspicion, and Tom said, "One thing he's got to learn is to turn his head toward you when you speak to him." Tom leaned over and stepped between the poles of the fence into the corral where the horse stood trembling and eying him with only the hackamore like a noose around his nose. "Learning some things is natural," and Tom grinned his wide, open smile, "but this one is like goin' to school and it's not even a little bit natural." Now his voice crooned along as he moved toward Sundance. "Not for him, it ain't. Hand me that whip, Pistol." A seven-foot whip with a rawhide tassel dangling from the slender end leaned against the corral fence, and this I handed to Tom. Standing very still, he held it down and waited, murmuring to Sundance, and when he stepped forward, Sundance turned to run off and Tom flicked his rear with the whip and turned him back. "See?" he whispered. "That's what I mean. We ain't goin' to do that, sweetheart. You turn your rump to me, and you're goin' to get stung. You keep lookin' at me when I walk up to you, and you won't. Okay? It's very easy." Again Sundance wheeled to race away and again the whip stung his rump. On the third try Sundance turned but thought better of it. "That's a boy," Tom sang, now close enough to hold the hackamore and rub his nose. "You catch on very fast. Now we'll just put a blanket on you and let you get used to that."

I brought the blanket across the corral for Tom to throw across his back, and we stood there rubbing his nose and his neck where the trembling muscles brought out dark patches of sweat.

"Pistol's goin' to be real old," Texas Diller drawled at the dinner table, "before he ever gets on that horse. Maybe as old as Seth, maybe older."

"You can't get no older than that," Red said.

"Driscoll's havin' himself a good time foolin' around with Pistol," Fonse said. "Leavin' us so shorthanded around chore time, I'm plumb wore out."

Sam laughed and I grinned to cover my nervousness, and Tom blinked at me and smiled a little while he crimped a cigarette, not bothered at all.

"Hell, I wouldn't nurse that horse or nobody," Red said. "I've broke more horses'n I can count, and I never would've finished the job doin' it this way." He shook his head, his burnished face scornful, and his pale eyes sought me out. "Pistol here'll get the idea you can treat any hunk of horseflesh this way."

I looked back to Tom where he held a big stove match to the end of his wet cigarette and drew in, his eyes on the match flame.

"The way to break a horse," Red continued, "is snub him and saddle him and ride him out till he gets some sense in his head and knows who's boss, and that's all there is to it."

And Texas Diller put in, "They don't do it no different in the Panhandle," and Fonse nodded. It was the way I had seen, too, and knew and heard about, and I glanced at Tom again. He had the little cigarette cupped in his hand and was blowing smoke toward the ceiling and watching it rise.

In the long pause I tried to muster an argument in support of Tom's way but I couldn't think of it right off, and in the silence Seth McCollum said, "I've broke 'em both ways," and instantly, intensely, everyone listened. "And I've rode 'em with no breakin' at all when I had to." The cowboys listened and watched the old face. "Some horses only bust one way, and that's rough, but gentlin' makes a better horse." A little silence followed and then a stirring in their chairs, but they didn't question Seth McCollum, and I knew the argument was ended.

In the evening I went back to the corral and talked to Sundance and brushed him down so that he would not be wet and sweaty through the night, and he shivered and shook under the currycomb and watched me always with fear and trembling.

Day by day Tom added one thing and then another to his education. The bridle replaced the hackamore, then the cold iron bit clanked against his teeth and pressed on his tongue. Then the full-rigged saddle with all its weight. The pressure of the cinch against his belly, pulled tighter and tighter day by day until at last it was secure enough to hold the saddle in place under the weight of a rider.

"Now," Tom said, "today, we'll just see what happens." He walked slowly to Sundance and talking to him all the time, he went very slowly through the routine of saddling him, pausing when he showed nervousness, waiting patiently, rubbing his nose and neck and always talking, and then in a flash so fast I scarcely saw it myself, he was in the saddle.

Sundance stood stock-still and shook, and then he burst away around the corral, but Tom held his head tight and high and pitted all his strength and weight and skill against the little maverick, and his last break for freedom came to nothing. Tom rode him around the great dusty corral while I watched, and when he came abreast of me, he grinned with great pleasure. "You've got a nice horse here, Pistol," he said, "a real nice little horse." When he came around again, he added, "You get a horse with spirit like this one, you don't want to break it or show him how to be mean, you want to use it. Then you got a horse," and his broad freckled face broke open in his wide wonderful grin, and I grinned, and we were both as pleased as two little kids.

Each day after that Tom drilled Sundance in the necessary skills of his existence as a cow horse and a roping pony, and he learned more and more quickly as he moved farther away from the memory of the wild buttes of other days until his skill was as much a pleasure to behold as his spirit and beauty and intelligence.

As Tom rode him one morning zigzag across the corral, teaching him the touch of the reins against his neck for left and right by shifting his two hundred pounds in the saddle, Red stuck his head and hat over the fence and watched and said, "You got a nice horse there, Pistol. It took till hell froze twice over but you got a horse."

"Now you try him for a bit, Pistol," Tom said. He held the bridle while I approached and mounted and watched me work him back and forth in the round enclosure.

"Okay," he said, "you're lookin' pretty good. To-morrow or the next day I think you can take him out."

My spirits rose up with a burst of laughter. Sundance was about to be mine.

As we walked away I said, "Red thinks it took too long this way."

"Yeah, but he learned it right and he knows all he got to know now, just fill it in with a little practice." Tom paused, grinning. "A whole lot of livin' is like horse breakin'. You get corralled and then you learn what you got to know and it's better to learn it gentle than learn it mean. Then you do it, and the ones that do it right are real pretty to watch."

The next day Tom asked Fonse to ride the little maverick and give him a hard ride. Tom himself was too big a man to ride the horse all day. Light and wiry Fonse worked the little animal until he was dark with sweat.

That evening at the supper table Sam said, "Is that horse about ready, Tom? We need to get going up to the summer range."

Tom nodded, much to my excitement. "Fonse rode him all day today," he said. "He looks good. I think Pistol can take him over." Then he grinned at me and added, "From now on he's all yours."

"Soon as we get his tail pulled," Roscoe said.

"We'll do that first thing, Pistol," Red said. "Then you can have him."

I grinned from ear to ear, hardly hearing Roscoe urge the tail pulling and clipping the mane. "It'll get in your eyes, Pistol," he said, "and you'll never get the horses in."

"Oh, Pistol's gettin' pretty quick," Texas said. "We're all ready to go by ten o'clock now."

I kept smiling with my teeth clenched and looked at Tom, who grinned back. No one was going to pull that little maverick's beautiful broomtail.

A discussion of work followed over the bitter coffee and tin cow and the crimped cigarettes, and it was decided that Tom would take me, Red, Fonse and Texas Diller up to the summer range the next day.

I rode Sundance that day, all day, for the entire trek into the high pines of the summer range. He skittered a good bit, rolling his eyes, tossing his head and snorting when I tried to mount, but I stuck with him and by evening he had given up such nonsense.

Saturday Night in Sunshine

5

"You crazy, Pistol?" Fonse said.

The rain pelted us. My shirt was stuck to my back and chest, and my Levi's were soaked through except where they hit the saddle leather, and my hat funneled steady streams like spouts front and back. Sundance hung his wet head down, his neck burdened by his heavy tangled mane and his sorrel coat darkened. We were close to drowning, and I sang at the top of my voice. I couldn't help it. After all those days of drought the sky had suddenly blackened, and it rained. Rain! The whole world smelled of pine needles and earth soaking up water. We didn't have slickers tied to our saddles. Who would think of them early on a dry, hot morning in the middle of a dry spell? Nobody, and so we were soaked to the skin and I was singing.

"Shut up, will you?" Fonse said. "You got the tune wrong. It goes 'O Danny boy,'" and in his sweet Irish tenor he sang it through as we trotted under the dripping pines.

The cow camp lay in an open meadow among the pine hills, an old log cabin chinked with white plaster, and a round pole corral with a halfhearted lean-to beside it. When we rode in, Tom was working in the corral, wearing a long yellow slicker slit up the rear to the hips but only reaching his calves because he was a tall man, and he gave us his big, wide wonderful grin and said, "Kind of feels good all the way around." Fonse sang even louder, and I laughed out loud. I cupped my hands together and let them fill with rain. Fame, fortune, love, adventure, name what you want most; it's not as precious as water in a thirsty land.

"I hope somebody drug my gear inside," Fonse said.

We hadn't used the old log cabin because it was dim and hot and reeked from decades of smoking fires and grease and the dens of generations of wild animals. But now the campfire in the open was black and abandoned, and somebody had dragged in all the bedrolls and duffles and the chuck box and cooking gear. The smell of wet saddle-worn clothes and men mingled with the older smells.

"I hope it don't rain long," Fonse said, as we stepped over the threshold, and Red turned on him, using the big stirring spoon like a weapon and yelled, "By God, if there's anything I hate it's a complainer." His long underwear which he wore all year round, the same suit for all I know, was soaked above the knee and across the shoulder blades it was plastered to his sizable muscles. Wet Levi's hung down steaming above the black iron cookstove, one pair dripping into the stewpot, but I decided against saying anything, since Red was very touchy about his cooking.

"I could use me a shot," Texas Diller said. The voices stopped short. Red stirred the stewpot absently. Fonse stood motionless, and from the peg where he hung his slicker, Tom turned his head and looked at Texas. An uneasiness filled me.

"Where you goin' to get it?" Red said.

"I know a fella," Texas said, "not too far off."

Again a little silence.

"Why don't you go see him?" Tom said. "You're all wet, anyhow."

"Yeah, get on it, Texas," Fonse said, hopping around, pulling off one boot.

"Don't mind if I do," Texas said, and settling his hat down on his forehead with a squidge, he took Tom's slicker which came to his ankles and left the cabin.

A great disquiet swept through me. I had seen enough drunken cowboys not to want to be penned in a dinky cabin with four of them. If a fight started, who would stop it? My only chance would be to escape outside. I listened. The wind and rain swept across the tin roof with their own uncontrollable violence. A branch beat against the metal. I could run for the lean-to, if I had to.

Supper came and went with nobody talking much, and while the others sat back and smoked in silence, I cleared up the bare plank table and washed the tin plates and tin cups and the stewpot over the cookstove. Tom dealt a hand of poker, and they played it out without speaking. Wind and rain continued to slash the cabin. While they studied a second hand, I unrolled my soogans next to the door. From there I figured I could get out fast.

An hour passed. Then two.

"What's keepin' him?" Red said.

"I wonder," Tom said sardonically.

"Maybe he's lost his sense of direction," Fonse said.

"Could be," Tom dealing again. "After this one I'm crawlin' in."

I slid between my homemade quilts and watched them warily as they finished the game and moved about the cabin, rolling out their beds. I was far too uneasy to sleep until I heard Tom say, "Better leave the lantern in the window." Then I faded away.

Two days later Texas Diller showed up. He rode into the pole corral that evening, and the deadpans were the deadest I have ever seen them. They acted as if Texas had never been away, and so did Texas. The needling began around the fire. "A shot sure feels good when you're wet," Fonse coughed consumptively. "I hope I get rid of this before I go under," and Texas looked very, very sad.

"My tooth is hurtin' me somethin' awful," he whimpered.

"I'm real sorry," Tom said.

Alternately I bled for Texas and choked trying not to laugh. They knew where the raw nerve lay, and they could stroke it with their knife wits forever, as I knew too well. They kept at it until Texas Diller unrolled his sleeping bag and pushed his way into it and put his hat over his face. Texas must have put a word in somewhere, because, when I drove the horses into camp the next morning, everybody had begun preparations.

The fire blazed, and Red had set the big washtub over it with a bar of homemade lye soap floating on top on a stick. Fonse sat on a log, spreading stove black on his boots and whistling mockingbird trills. With a boot in one hand Texas Diller stared at his toes as he wiggled them painfully.

"What's up?" I said.

Tom brought a rumpled, slightly gray white shirt to the fire, and Red rubbed the collar and the cuffs and the armpits with the lye soap and stirred it into the tub.

"This kid is gettin' pretty smart," Red said to him. "How come he don't know there's a dance tonight in Sunshine?"

"Maybe nobody told him," Tom said.

Red nodded gravely, stirring. "Where's your shirt, Alfonso?"

Fonse pulled back the canvas on his bedroll and shook out a black and white checked shirt and black and white checked pants to match. He even had a wire hanger which he hung from a tree. Red stopped stirring. Tom and Texas exchanged glances.

"Well," Texas said, "I don't hardly know what to say."

Singing merrily Fonse danced a circle two-step around the fire.

When the shirts had boiled, Red raised them one by one on his stick and passed them out. Tom took his away from the immediate camp and stretched and patted it out in the sun on the dry grass.

They hadn't seen booze or women for weeks, no one but Texas, anyway. I knew what kind of a dance it would be. I took my shirt and followed Tom away from camp.

"Somebody ought to stay here, Tom. I mean. That steer's pretty sick. I can stay. I don't mind."

"Why?" Tom said.

"I'm not much of a dancer. I don't go to a lot of dances in town. I'd just as soon . . ."

Tom put a stone on his shirttail to secure it against the wind. I did, too. Tom smiled, "You'll get into it. If you need a little boost, I'll be there."

That afternoon when everybody had shaken out his stiffened white shirt and climbed into the cleaner of his Levi's and Fonse was dressed in his checkered suit with a red tie and his boots shined with stove black, Texas Diller sat down on the log and cried out, "I can't make it, boys, I just can't make it. You go ahead and have a good time. My tooth's hurtin' me so's I can't hardly think."

"I've had about enough of that tooth," Red said. "I guess we got to shoot him."

"I can't hurt no more than I do," Texas said, "so go ahead, shoot."

"Maybe you could pull it," I said, and they turned, staring at me. "Maybe with some pliers."

"Now there, there, Pistol's got something, Tom. I told you this kid is gettin' smart. I always kind of hankered to be a dentist."

Texas jumped up from the log and looked wildly around him. "You ain't goin' to touch a tooth of my head," he yelled. Tom settled him back against the log, saying, "Yes, we are, Texas, you just sit still. I'm goin' to administer the anesthetic."

Texas pushed upwards, yelling, "Don't you touch me. You hit me one, Driscoll, and I'll die on ya. You'll go up for murder." Tom pushed him down on the log again

57

and patted his cheek, saying. "Naturally you're nervous, Doctor understands."

Slowly, carefully, Red stepped over the bedrolls and opened Texas's canvas and reached in and pulled out a Mason jar of potato moonshine, and while Texas stared, forlorn, Red loosened the two-piece Ball lid, passed the open mouth under his nose, swished a mouthful thoughtfully and nodded.

Watching the moonshine go down, I felt my stomach sink with it. This was going to be some dance, if we ever got there, which I hoped we wouldn't.

"It's important to do this right," Red said, tasting again. "Pistol, scrape up that fire and heat up the coffee."

I did as I was told.

Red passed the Mason jar to Fonse who took a swig and handed it to Tom who tasted it critically and gave it to Texas. "Drink up," Tom said, "and you won't feel a thing."

Texas drank, six or seven long gulps, without coughing or blinking or stopping, while Red stood over the last of the fire, holding the pliers in the blackened coffee pot. Fonse settled himself on Texas's legs.

"I can still feel it," Texas cried. "More anesthetic."

"More anesthetic," Red commanded. They passed the jar again, last of all to the patient.

Then Red pulled the pliers from the pot and waved them in the air. "Everything is now sanitary and we are ready to operate," he said, approaching Texas, who was now lying on the ground with his head held against the log in Tom's two big hands.

"Which one is it?" Red asked.

"It's way back," Texas whimpered. "Oh, I can still feel the pain."

"I can't feel a thing," Red said. "Open up. Wide. Wider. Which one?"

"Way back," came the whisper, and Red stuffed the pliers inside, clamped them on and pulled and hollered, "I got one! I got one!" And a tooth came out. He stared at it. Tom let go of Texas's head, and Fonse rolled off his feet, and Texas sat up, spitting blood. "But did I get the right one?" Red asked.

"I don't know yet," Texas said. He rinsed his mouth with moonshine.

"It was the only one back there I could see," and Red and Tom hoisted Texas to his feet and propelled him to his horse.

"If my foot starts hurtin'," Texas said, "you ain't goin' to operate on no leg of mine."

"If your foot starts hurtin'," Red said, mounting, "you better not let me know it. I kind of go for this doctorin'."

The five of us, bunched together, turned our horses and set off at a fast trot across the hills and coulees toward Sunshine. Texas held the nearly empty Mason jar in the crook of his right arm as he rode, and for once he was silent. Every so often he spat and swished his mouth with moonshine and swallowed. No one said anything much to him, but Tom kept an eye on him.

The sun set and darkness settled in before we saw the little clutch of frame buildings which was Sunshine. Red let out a whoop, the rest of us whooped and hollered and whipped up the horses for the last dash downhill into town. For all the noise we made, we could still hear the sawed-off strains of "Whispering" coming out of the dance hall.

Model A's and battered pickups were parked all around the community house. Dozens of horses were tied, unsaddled, to the hitching rails; mounds of saddles and saddle blankets were set around under the cotton-woods. We set up such a commotion arriving that cowboys came to the big open double door and scrambled out onto the porch, peering into the darkness.

"Two quarts it's Tom and the boys," I heard someone say. There were no takers, because we were already unsaddled and rushing the steps.

The hall was a two by four and bare board structure, its unpainted sides left to weather in sun and snow. A big double door opened onto the porch in front which we now climbed up to the whistles and whoops and greetings of other punchers. Just inside the door each of us paid a dollar to Seth McCollum who sat behind a kitchen table. Benches lined the bare walls all the way around, with pegs above them for hats; in one corner a little kitchen was set up; and halfway down one side on a raised platform three men played their instruments, an ancient upright piano, a country fiddle, and a mail order clarinet. When they stopped playing, the cowboys whooped and hollered and stamped and whisked their partners back to the benches along the wall. The band immediately struck up "Five Foot Two, Eyes of Blue," and Fonse sang, "Oh de-do-de-dody-doo," and made for the women's side.

I hung back against the wall, wondering and watching. Tom spun by, dancing with Lacey, and how that man could dance. He whirled with a lightness and grace even the wiry Fonse couldn't match. All the cowboys

danced fast and surely and well. Stamping and hollering, they spun past me. Fonse was jerked onto the
bandstand to sing, and I moved into the crowd in front
to watch and yelled till the dusty rafters rocked to the
whooping, although he wasn't really that good. Then
the fiddler shouted, "Everybody take your partner,
circle two-step!" The cheering whooped up again, and
old Seth McCollum left his seat behind the kitchen
table. His white hair shining in the yellow light, a little
smile of pleasure on his leather-brown face, he circled
the floor alone with Mrs. Gallagher. There was a great
cheer again, the others grabbed their partners and filled
the floor. All the women had partners, little girls of
nine, old ladies of fifty. Dancing with all the ranch
women was an unspoken courtesy which every man
observed. Besides, there weren't enough young ones to
go around.

"Come on, Pistol," Fonse hollered as he spun by, his
small black-booted feet making little running steps between the beat. I grinned and stirred, thinking I could
start with Mrs. Gallagher and get warmed up and then
maybe try Lacey Barnett, if I could get close to her.

Texas Diller slid off the bench and stretched out on
the floor beside me. He didn't move. I squatted beside
him and looked into the half-open, pink-glazed eyes, and
I knew he wasn't going to move. I got him under the
arms and dragged him to the open doors while the
people nearby laughed and the punchers hooted and I
grinned grimly, pulling him across the porch and down
the steps, his heels striking the planks with hollow
thumps as he went. I hauled him as far as the big cottonwood tree, and there I staked him out and stood there a
minute, wondering. The music stopped, and the stamp-

ing and hooting and hollering greeted the silence. The patch of bright doorway darkened as the punchers rushed through and outside onto the porch and into the yard. They were swarming all around me, pulling the Mason jars of potato moonshine out of saddlebags and the backs of pickups and the rumble seats of Model A's. "Have a swig," and somebody pressed the jar into my hand and I held it up, pretending. Just the smell was enough to make you blink, and I coughed and spluttered as if I had taken a swallow, and they laughed, pounding me on the back and hollering, "Attaboy," and, "That's good old Montana rotgut," and when the jar got to Dominic Arlo, he drained it and flung it high and wide with a great bellowing whoop followed by a moment of silence while everybody waited to hear it crash against the hard earth somewhere out in the dark, which brought on another triumphant cowboy yell.

Now the music struck up again and I followed the bunch back in, feeling strange and uneasy. The men were drunk and getting drunker. I went straight for Tom.

"Tom," I said, "I laid Texas out . . ." His eyes swept over me without recognition. His arm swung out and brushed me aside like a branch that hung in his way as he made for the benches where the women sat. I stood still with my mouth open for a second, with the feeling coming up in me that I felt when an unchecked herd thundered too close to me, when I held the calf for the routine cruelties of branding and castrating, events I knew were part of the life, a part I wasn't sure I either liked or wanted. Then I saw Allison Mitchell in the doorway. I closed my mouth.

62

Allison Mitchell was a girl I knew from school because her family moved into town in the winter, and she summered on the family place next to Sam's. I didn't know her very well. She was just there, that was all, but now she looked pretty good. She was almost as tall as I was and very thin with a tiny bony face and she wore her dark hair wrapped in two squawlike braids that made her look about ten years old. Stroking his walrus moustache next to her, stood her father, Terence Mitchell, the remittance man, dressed in dusty brown pants and a great brown and white plaid jacket with patch pockets, something, I figured, sent over from England with his remittance. Going toward her, I wished Allison had her hair curled up in fat rolls like Lacey Barnett. You just looked more of a girl that way, but Allison was somebody to dance with. I hesitated. Tom stamped by with the Widow Garrison, his face stony blank. Red, scowling, was right behind him. I took a deep breath. Allison smiled in delight when she saw me. Mr. Mitchell gripped my hand with a grin, "Thank God somebody's sober," he said.

I stamped on her feet halfway around the room before she said, "Are you working out here, Billy?" and I said, "Yup," and she said, "Where are you working?" and I said, "Tolliver's." We circled the floor twice before either of us could think of anything more. I began to see some of the advantages of moonshine. Nobody who was drinking it had trouble saying anything.

"We're up on the summer range right now," I said. "We had to ride ten miles to get here."

"Oh," she said, and after a while, "that's a long way."

63

"Yup," I said. Two times around and then, "We had to doctor one of the boys before we could leave camp."

She looked troubled. "Was he sick?"

"He had a toothache."

"What did you do?"

I told her the story which sent her into gales of laughter which loosened me up quite a bit and made her seem much older than she seemed when her face was still.

Red whooped by us, hollering, "Attaboy, Pistol," and I blushed and stiffened up again and could think of nothing more to say.

After I took Allison back to her father where he stood talking to Seth and thanked her for the dance, I was headed straight for Lacey Barnett when I was almost knocked flat by Allie Bassett so that I missed out. Lacey looked over his shoulder as they spun away and smiled and formed the words, "Next time, Billy." I felt much better and danced with Mrs. Gallagher, and while we were dancing, I determined to ask Lacey for the supper dance.

The supper dance was the important dance of the night. You tried to get it with the most popular girl or the one you liked best, because then you had that dance together and then supper and afterwards another dance. When I got to Lacey for the next dance, she was saying to half a dozen cowboys, "No, I promised this one to Billy Catlett," tossing her head of sausage curls.

They gave me the works as I pushed through them with Lacey smiling and saying, "You're just jealous of Billy." I danced her away as quickly as I could. After circling the floor once I asked her if she had promised anyone the supper dance yet, and she looked very disappointed and brushed my shoulder with her left hand, saying, "Oh, darn it, Billy, why didn't you say something an hour ago? I'd just love to sit with you, but I've already promised Allie Bassett. He asked me the first thing, and I didn't want to be left sitting all my myself so I promised him, but if I hadn't, I'd just love to have it with you."

She was lying, but she made me feel good just the same. Looking away, I saw the little face of Allison Mitchell, very sad and serious, twirling by, and I felt sorry for her. She just didn't know how to make a fellow relax and feel good like Lacey. Maybe that was why, between the next dances, I asked her for the supper dance. I saw myself doing for her what Lacey did for me.

In the middle of the next circle two-step the stamping and hollering rose to a wild pitch. "Clear the floor," somebody yelled. "Get 'em out of here," Sam roared. Red was in a fight with Dominic Arlo. They swung wildly at each other, never landing a blow. The women climbed up on the benches to see better, and the men milled around Dominic and Red, pushing and shoving, until they ushered them onto the porch where Red and Dominic promptly fell down the steps and Sam closed the big double doors, shot the bolt and turning, raised his arms like a band leader. The band struck up, and Seth McCollum led Mrs. Gallagher again to the floor and they circled swiftly, hip to hip, to the sawed-off, tinny strains.

About midnight the crowd began to thin out. The little kids were put to bed in the cars and trucks parked outside. The cowboys began to disappear. Most of them were out cold under the cottonwoods in back. Only the sturdy dance lovers kept on after midnight. The young ranchers and their wives and the boys and girls kept whirling on with the fiddler sawing away.

I came back again and again to Allison Mitchell until I danced with her all the time. She had caught onto my dancing, finally. At least I wasn't hitting her toes, and when I did a turn, she went with me, and all of a sudden it was a pleasure, like riding a horse, when you and the rhythm of the horse are going together. With my arm around her waist and her thin brown arm on my shoulder we moved together, feeling the beat and the movement and Allison smiling at me and I was grinning and I realized that we didn't have to say much because what we had to say was coming out another way.

Close to 4:00 A.M. signs of breaking up appeared, which sent Allie Bassett swiftly around the room passing his hat for the benefit of the band. They played another hour. Then someone passed his hat again for another half hour, and then another, until dawn lit the sky outside.

When I saw Allison Mitchell off in the car with her father, she put her hand over mine where her father couldn't see her, and said, "I had a wonderful time," and smiled, and I smiled and when she smiled, she looked as much of a girl as Lacey in spite of her Indian braids. I watched them drive away and when I turned, I thumped into Tom. He didn't say anything, but he was vertical, and in silence we saddled the horses. I took care of Sundance and then saddled Red's horse and Fonse's while Tom picked them up from the ground by a fistful of shirt front and stuck their heads in the watering trough and gave them a leg up into the saddle.

When we reached camp, I stirred up the fire and pulled the blackened pot over the flame.

"Whatcha doin', Pistol, for Chrissake?" Fonse said.

"Fixing breakfast," I said. He turned his head away.

Tom sat down on the log and rubbed his hair.

"Do you want some breakfast, Tom? I can fix it for you."

He shook his head, not looking up. "Just some coffee, Pistol. I'll doctor that steer before I turn in."

"I'll give you a hand," I said.

Afterwards we crawled into our soogans and slept all day Sunday.

In Great Plain

6

Before we came down from the summer range, the nights had turned chill, and the kiss of autumn already yellowed the cottonwoods along the upper creeks. As we came down the hills, trailing the herd before us, Red said, "This whole country is either goin' to burn up or blow away or both."

"It looks like no rain around here anywhere," Tom said.

"What're these critters goin' to live on all winter?" Fonse wondered. "There isn't enough to keep 'em right now."

"They're caught between a rock and a hard place," Red said.

Tom shook his head, saying, "Maybe Sam'll have to sell off most of them."

"Everybody's goin' to be sellin'." And Tom nodded.

The drought now was serious. It was too late for rain,

because the growing season was past. Now we faced the winter. It was a question of survival.

Sam was not at the main ranch when we got in one midafternoon. Only Mrs. Gallagher was there. Lacey, she said, had gone back home to Lame Deer. I wandered from my bedroom into the living room to the kitchen. Outside, the wind whipped and whined, beating dirt like pellets against everything that faced it. Seated across from her at the long oilclothed dinner table I helped Mrs. Gallagher peel apples for pies.

"Whose pictures are those in the living room?" I asked her.

"What pictures?" she said.

"The ones on the table under the front window."

"Oh, those." She looked displeased. "That's Mrs. Tolliver."

"Who's the boy?"

"That's their son."

"Are they dead or something?"

"They live in California. I guess this is too rough a life for the likes of her." Mrs. Gallagher turned her back on me and washed the apples in the sink.

"Kind of lonely, I guess," I said, and I felt the loneliness, too, the wind crying.

I carried in armloads of wood for the woodbox next to the cookstove and started the works in the carbide light house so that the pump under the house would work and filled the bucket beside the washbasin on the porch before the little Model A bounced down the hill and pulled up in front of the kitchen door. Sam grinned when he saw me and put his arm around my shoulders and greeted me, "Howdy, Pistol," with such apparent pleasure that the loneliness I felt in the whining, pellet-laden wind fell away, and Mrs. Gallagher called out, "You can ring the triangle, Billy, now that Sam's here," and I struck the iron triangle hanging from the roof of the porch until the racket filled the gray world around me. The punchers came up from the bunkhouse, hats pulled down, shoulders hunched, hands pushed into tight pockets, leaning against the wind.

The talk that night turned around how many head of cattle could winter on what grass was left. The steers that were ready, of course, the ones of the right age and weight, were scheduled for sale, but this year maybe more should be sold. Estimates went back and forth. Roscoe thought the grass lower down would hold some, and Tom queried him on how it looked, and Sam reported the talk around the feedlots in town where he had been that day. In a moment's silence Seth McCollum said, "I never saw it like this before." With those words he made my mind an avenue of the autumns he had spent on these prairies, wet and dry, cold and unseasonably hot, windy and still, empty and peopled, the autumns of the buffalo dissolving into the autumn of the longhorn, autumns before barbed wire and after.

Sam listened and considered, and after the meal was cleared away and the men had gone out and Mrs. Gallagher sat at the end of the table with one last cup of coffee, he spread his account book in front of him and scratched his grizzled gray hair. Dead beat but reluctant to leave, I sat down nearby, watching while he made calculations on empty pages at the back of the book until he looked up and said, "Well, Pistol, I guess I'll have to run you into town the end of the week."

"This week?"

"I saw your dad today and he thinks you'd better come in and get ready for school."

"Gee, it isn't that time yet, is it? It can't be."

"Tom says you've been a pretty good horse wrangler."

"I hope so. I sure hope so. I've learned a lot from Tom, Sam," I said.

"I don't know a better man to learn from. We'll be needing a wrangler again next summer, so if you need a job and want to come out . . ."

"I'll take it," I said. Mrs. Gallagher laughed, and Sam laughed, reaching out and tousling my head roughly and saying, "Pistol," nothing more.

I said good-by to Tom and the other hands and stowed my gear in the rumble seat of Sam's Model A coupe, and he drove me into town.

Nobody came out of the house when we pulled up, and Sam said, "I guess they've forgotten you, Pistol," and I said, "Yeah," kind of laughing but not much as I pulled out my duffle and saddle and bedroll and let them drop to the curb. Sam said, "Got everything?" looking at me as if from a distance through his flickering hawk's eyes, and I said, "I guess." Then he moved brusquely, gripping my hand and saying, "See you down at the pens when we bring the herd in," and circled the car and got in and drove away, never looking back.

The house, the old four-square, two-story, frame house, still didn't open up, and it looked, well, drab. It was just an empty box compared to Sam's main ranch with the low white buildings snuggled into the hollows against the wind.

When I opened the front door, Conrad was lying on the living room couch reading the *Saturday Evening Post*.

"Howdy, puncher," he said without moving.

"I thought maybe you had all lit out while I was gone."

"No such luck."

"Boy, I had a great time out at Sam's, Conrad."

"That one-horse outfit." And so it began. Whenever I brought it up, he told a better story about Kincaid's. Whatever I said about Sam's, Kincaid's was better. I quit trying and kicked myself for being so stupid that I had to learn all over again to keep what I valued out of his sight.

Even my father, when he came home that night from the dogger plant, seemed not much more interested. I didn't feel like telling him, anyway, as I watched him settle into his chair in his three-button oatmeal sweater and his runover moccasin slippers, unfolding the paper. Next to the vigor of Tom and Red, their lithe physiques, tanned faces, flickering eyes, he appeared a pale city man. He wouldn't understand.

Even my mother couldn't compare with Mrs. Gallagher's heartiness. She was so thin and nervous and worried all the time that a clattering saucepan made her jump. She wanted to hear about Sam's, though; she wanted to know if I had been sick, had I changed my underwear, had the food been good, had I worked hard and done everything I was told to do, which made me burst out laughing. I told her little things, half teasing, in the kitchen before dinner. Tom and Sundance, what was important, I kept to myself. Anyway, home didn't matter too much after I got used to it; school started.

On the first morning Conrad and I set out at a fast walk and picked up Sonny Goldstein as we went through the business district, and he said, "I heard

Coach didn't come back," and we said, no, I don't believe it, protesting that no such disaster could happen until Richie Greatbear joined up as we crossed the NP tracks. He said, "It's true. The new coach was at the Laurel one night when I was selling papers." General silence. "He's called Buskirk or something, from Chicago." We spit a few obscene words through our teeth and turned off through the knot of orange railroad workers' shacks where from one Raf Gomez stepped out, calling, "Hallo, gringoes."

"Jees, did you hear about Coach?" and at the news Raf's face saddened so abruptly that we broke out laughing.

His name wasn't Buskirk, and I was the first to know. When I slid into the screwed-down desk in my first class, which was English, and finally quit looking around the room, I saw his name written carefully on the blackboard. "Mr. Burbank." And the man with his hands folded on the desk and the curled-up happy smile on his face, that was the new football coach. He strolled up and down; he told us where he came from, Chicago, a big high school, Nicholas Senn or Fenn or something, and he had to get away from the city for his health. He told us what he was going to teach and how pleased he was that he could use that great book *Giants in the Earth* as an example of the novel, and he wanted to get into it right now. He opened his copy and began to read, " 'There were giants in the earth in those days; and also after that, when the sons of God came in unto the daughters of men, and they bare children to them, the same became mighty men which were of old, men of renown.' "

"And what is that quotation from?" he asked, and

nobody knew but Allison Mitchell, who raised her slim brown hand like a leaf waving in the wind. "Genesis, of course." Burbank smiled his curled-up smile and went on. " 'Chapter One. Toward the Sunset. Bright, clear sky over a plain so wide that the rim of the heavens cut down on it around the entire horizon . . . Bright clear sky, today, tomorrow, and for all time to come.' " I felt a prickling thrill go over me. He read on: " 'And sun! And still more sun! It set the heavens afire every morning; it grew with the day to quivering golden light — then softened into all the shades of red and purple as evening fell. Pure colour everywhere. A gust of wind, sweeping across the plain, threw into life waves of yellow and blue and green. Now and then a dead black wave would race over the scene . . . a cloud's gliding shadow . . . now and then . . .' " My body was rigid with listening, yes, that's the way it was, that writer was telling the truth, I knew, I knew, but he was reading on, " '. . . a small caravan . . . a stocky, broad-shouldered man . . . behind them a team of oxen . . . this was the caravan of Per Hansa . . . moving west to Dakota Territory. There he intended . . .' "

Hack Davis jumped up. "The goddam honyocker," he yelled. "Boy, that's the trouble with this country. The goddam honyockers move in and rip up the grass and try to dry farm it." The chorus of assent rose with him, and Mr. Burbank stood transfixed. "I'm not going to listen to any goddam book about honyockers. Boy, wait'll my father hears about this." Hack's father owned the newspaper, a position, we believed, of power and reason.

Mr. Burbank's mouth was opening and closing like a fish as the bell shrilled and the room emptied in disgust, leaving only Allison who wanted to know how much she should read for tomorrow. I hung back by the door kind of feeling sorry for the guy and wondering if I shouldn't tell him what hit him. This way nobody'd go out for football.

"Do you agree with Hack?" Allison watched me.

"Well, I . . ."

"What if it is about honyockers? What's wrong with that? Honyockers have just as much right to be in a book as anybody else. Cowpunchers, for instance."

"Well, yeah, okay," I said, "but who's going to believe that around here?"

She glared at me, her little brown face dark with anger, and then she laughed. "Well, I don't care," she said, "I'm going to read it. It sounds wonderful to me."

By three-thirty Mr. Burbank sat at his desk, staring at the floor between his shoes, a beaten man.

"My name's Billy Catlett," I said, and he nodded. "You probably never heard of a honyocker back in Chicago, but a honyocker is a dryland farmer and . . ."

"Somebody told me third period," he said.

"Well, it's pretty dry out here right now and everybody's worried and they blame their troubles . . ." He looked up at me and I said, "Billy Catlett, I'm in your first-period class," and he nodded. "Besides, nobody ever did like them much."

"Why?" he asked, and for the life of me I couldn't think of a really good reason.

The next morning when I slid sideways into my desk and whispered to Hack, "What'd your dad say?" he said, "No use making a big stink, the book's paid for, or words to that effect." I looked at Mr. Burbank, who sat here just like yesterday with his hands folded at his desk and smiling his curled-up smile, looking not at all beaten.

"Before we go further with Per Hansa," he said, and the class eyed him deadpan, "I want to assign some written work. I'd like to know just where you are with written expression," and he smiled, facing us, "I know where you are with oral expression." Nobody laughed. "Now this assignment is due on Friday, and it can be anything, a poem, an essay, a story, a report, but there is only one subject and I am assigning the subject for all of you. The subject is honyockers," and his voice went on and on, asking for trouble, and I knew there wasn't any way to help him, that I might just as well sit back and watch him get it.

Hack said he wasn't going to write anything for the big lunkheaded dude, and I was thinking the same thing, rummaging in my locker after school when I heard Allison say, "Billy," and I said, "Yeah," very offhand, wondering what was the matter with her, anyway, didn't she know girls didn't go to boys' lockers, and she said, "What are you going to write?" and she looked so sad and worried that I said, "Well, a sort of a story, I guess."

"Do you know any honyockers?"

"Sure," I said, annoyed. "Who doesn't?"

"I don't," she said.

I looked at her, wondering, and said, "You're real good on quotations," which sounded meaner than I expected and I added, "The Shotlicks are honyockers."

"The people with the vegetable stand?" She brightened. "I could stop there and talk to Mrs. Shotlick. Oh, Billy, you're wonderful."

"Well, who's that?" Conrad hissed in my ear, and I said, "Who'd ya mean?" knowing very well, and he said, "You know who, that one?"

"Oh, Allison Mitchell," I muttered, and he hitched up his pants and swelled his chest, saying, "I say, she's a little bit of all right," and swaggered past her, looking into her eyes, and I saw her face flush, and my stomach sank.

Never did I hate and admire Conrad more than that moment when he cased Allison Mitchell, a girl who up to that moment I didn't even know I cared about.

The call for football went out before school Friday, and we gathered by the battered radiator where the first floor halls came together and Sonny said, "Does anybody want to play for him?" in his earnest and worried way. And Richie said, "He makes me think of an elder out on the reservation, very old man," and he laughed his deep, easy, affectionate laugh.

"Very old man makes very poor coach," Raf said, as Conrad scowled sourly.

On Monday morning Mr. Burbank moved down the rows, passing papers this way and that, reaching across to one person and turning around for the next, and smiling with his curled-up lips. "Allison," handing out her paper. "Bill Catlett." I took the paper, slipping into my desk, and got settled and composed a deadpan face because I could see that it said right under the title, "The Honyocker Kid," A—. I'd never had an A— in my life, and under it in Burbank's little up-and-down hand was written, "Excellent! Your story has told me a lot of things I didn't know before: about cattle drives, about cowboys, about prairies, and about the honyocker kid and what he does and how he acts and why nobody likes him. What's more, you have used your own language, which suits the subject. You have also used your own spelling, which is entirely too original."

Well. Maybe I would go out for football.

I spent the fall on the practice field as part of the team the first string tackled. When I got into the showers and inspected the day's bruises, Richie Great-bear said, "You show plenty coup, little white brother," and then laughed his open, affectionate laugh. He helped a little to heal my wounds, which were more than surface ones. Conrad inflicted a lot of them. He was the star.

Some mornings I didn't hang around the radiator but slipped into Burbank's room to follow some unfinished thought from days before. We pursued Emerson for a long time. Burbank was very enthusiastic about Emerson. Emerson, he said, had made the break toward original American ideas. He had called on Americans to trust themselves. I argued that trusting ourselves came long before, with Columbus even, and that no one would have left Europe if they hadn't. Those days were like out here. If you didn't trust yourself, you wouldn't come, and you sure wouldn't stay.

"Good point," Mr. Burbank said. "Either we had self-reliance, or self-reliance was thrust upon us. However, saying it, stating the idea, is more important than it sounds."

I never mentioned our discussions because the other guys thought Burbank was kind of ridiculous, and he was different but not ridiculous. He listened to what you had to say and made you feel it was worthwhile to say it.

Saturdays were best of all. They were edged with silver, opening in frost and closing in frost. Between, the sun was hot, the air cold, and the earth still warm.

On the sagebrush flats where the two rivers joined, flocks of sage grouse gathered. We knew they were there, those beautiful, succulent, dumb chickens, and we pursued them. Our .22's dangling, bolts open, Richie and Sonny and I strode abreast to the edge of town and cut through the hay fields and corn patches of the small-time farmers. All the time Sonny argued earnestly for survival of the fittest, which he had just heard about. I couldn't see it. Weren't we after the plumpest young adults, intending to take nature's best selections if we could? Richie said that men were part of nature's intention.

"Men with guns?" Sonny said, serious and surprised.

"A gun to a man is like a claw to a bear or speed to a cat," Richie said, and you could see the animal wariness already on him. "Better circle downwind."

We moved down the ridge, avoiding the path of the sun, and came through the flats upright as far as we dared. Then we spread out, and I dropped behind a clump of brush. I waited, listening. The kuk-kuk-kuk continued from the same place with no sound of wings. I crawled closer on my hands and knees. The warmth of earth and scent of sage surrounded me. I peered around an outcropping of rock and saw the flock still feeding through the stubble. Snaking forward on my belly, I made the next sagebrush. One flew up, and the others followed, flapping a hundred yards and settling down again over the meadow to forage and kuk-kuk about. I waited. They calmed down, and I wormed my way toward them.

79

Suddenly Richie fell on me and pinned me to the ground. I swore at him. "You're a big hunter," I snarled, "mighty red man," and I cussed again.

Fifteen feet away, rising from his belly, Sonny fired.

"Get off, you big ape."

Richie refused. "Don't move," he whispered.

The birds were alert now. I would never get a shot. Sonny crouched and fired again. Now he was standing and pulling the bolt. "What's the matter with you guys? Come on."

"Look straight ahead," Bear said.

I picked my face out of the stubble and looked. Before me, not eighteen inches from my eyes, a diamondback rattlesnake lay coiled in the sagebrush. His wide-open black bead eye regarded me. The sweat burst out of my body, and I began to shake. On top of me Bear relaxed.

"Why didn't you say so?"

"I did, Cat, soon as you got through cussing."

Sonny ran after the flock as they rose and kuk-kuked frantically and took wing. "Come on," he yelled. "You can still get some."

My shirt was soaked with sweat and shivers racked me. Richie got to his feet. Finally alerted to the danger, the birds had flown into the cottonwood brakes along the river. We backed out of the rattler's range, and I sat up.

"Look." Sonny held up his bag. "I got seven. Not bad, huh? What happened to you guys, anyway? What were you doing on top of Cat? You looked so funny I nearly missed a shot."

Richie pointed his gun barrel to the rattler still coiled in the sagebrush.

"Oh, my God!" Sonny sat down suddenly beside me.

"Why didn't you shoot him? You should have shot him, Rich."

"Then there would be no birds."

"Yeah, that's right. At least I got some. No use spoiling it for everybody. Well, I'm going to shoot him now."

"Why?" Richie said. "He didn't hurt anybody."

"Cowboys always kill a rattler when they find one," I said, still shaking. "One bite can finish a calf."

"A medicine man told me snakes carry messages to the gods below the earth. They never kill one. They think if they did, they might keep a prayer from getting to the right place."

"What kind of prayers?" I asked.

"To make things grow."

"I can't see that a snake could say anything good about anything," Sonny said.

"Still, if they make things grow, we can use some help," I said. I wiped my face on my sleeve and laughed with relief.

"This sure wrecks my survival of the fittest argument," Sonny said. "I'd like to see somebody make a theory out of this expedition."

"Go hunting with your buddies," I said, and we laughed.

"But that's a moral," Sonny said, and I said, "And it leaves out the snake. Burbank wants us to tie in everything."

"O snake," Richie said, laughing, "tell the story of the three friends out hunting to the gods below," and laughing, we saluted the snake still coiled in the sagebrush, his black bead eye open on the world.

Saturday afternoons I warmed the bench at the football game. Only there isn't any way to keep the bench warm in Montana. I huddled under two army blankets and watched Bear at first-string tackle. Sonny went in and out at right end, alternating with Hack Davis. Raf ran like a rabbit at left half. And Conrad called the plays. I couldn't help admiring him. He had learned how and had practiced, and, one thing for certain, he was real pretty to watch.

When I heard Sam had brought the herd in, I ran down to the stockyards and made my way through the runways until I saw Tom's familiar black hat bobbing above the top rail. When he saw me, he grinned his wide, wonderful grin and said, "Howdy, Pistol, how's it goin'?" and Sam joined us by the fence, and I said, "Did you bring in a big herd?"

"The regular lot," Sam said. "I'm going to try to get through. I'm buying up feed, cottonseed cake, here and there, to get by. If the winter isn't too bad, we'll make it."

The winter set in early and severely. Shortly after the killing frosts a blizzard struck. The wind came down out of the northwest laden with dry snow. Clouds of it, blinding, stinging masses, whipped into my face, burning and freezing my cheeks between home and school. This snow melted and ran off the frozen earth, helping very little to alleviate the drought. Another snow hit. As the weeks went by, it promised to be one of the worst winters Montana had ever known.

Christmas on Wolf Creek

7

I had delivered the afternoon prescriptions for Acton's drugstore, where I had picked up an after-school job, hurrying up Main Street before it grew dark and colder. The store windows glittered with Christmas lights, and the snow was shoveled into huge windrows at the outer edge of the sidewalk. I was thinking about stopping for a hamburger before going home to dinner when I saw Sam coming toward me on the street.

Just seeing him made me feel good, and watching him, I thought, if I ever had to be fifty, I wanted to look like Sam. He carried himself erect and springy, and he looked heavier than he was, buttoned into his soiled sheepskin coat. His hat brim had more of a roll on the right side than the left, because that was the way he ran his free hand along it when he lifted his hat to wipe his forehead on his sleeve or maybe just ease the sweatband.

When he saw me, his rough face didn't change expression. It just warmed up and he held out his hand

and greeted me and called me Pistol, and I felt good as if I had suddenly by accident dropped into the right hole, and then he asked me what I was doing with school out and if I wanted to come out to the ranch for a few days and help Tom drive a herd over to Wolf Creek where he had been able to stock feed for them. The herd was already quartered at Tom's place, so the drive would only be about ten miles, not a big day's work. Red was in the Wolf Creek camp, looking after another herd, and Tom and I would drive the rest over there.

Sam knew there wasn't much question whether I wanted to or not, just would my parents let me go and I could leave a message for him at the Marshall House when I found out. I raced home to find my mother who said it was all right so long as I was home by Christmas and dressed warmly. I hauled my saddle and heavy leather chaps to the front porch and stowed my extra shirts and pants and mitten liners and overshoes, which fitted over my high-heeled boots, into a duffle bag with my razor, which I didn't need yet, and I was ready, prancing, when next morning Sam appeared in his Model A coupe.

The road was covered in snow. The loose layers had blown off, leaving bare the tracks which had been beaten into the frozen surface. The day was gray and still and cold, and the trip passed swiftly enough as we discussed, man to man, the seriousness of range conditions and what the future might hold.

The herd was quartered halfway between Sam's main ranch and Wolf Creek at Tom's place, and we went there to prepare for the drive. Tom had a modest spread and ran his cattle with Sam's and worked for Sam. The little house was dominated by a radio with a gigantic horn which brought in Dr. Brinkley loud and clear.

"By God, this place is a pigpen, Driscoll. You need to get a woman in here somehow," Sam said, and Tom rubbed his hair, laughing. It struck me funny, too, to think of Tom with a woman, a wife, maybe kids. To me he was perfect and complete when he was on his horse working cattle on the open range.

Early the next morning we got ready for the drive. I put on my long underwear, wool pants, Levi's and chaps and a work shirt and a wool shirt and melton cloth mackinaw and melton cloth Scotch cap that had a flap from ear to ear, boots and rubber-soled felt over-shoes and my big mittens with two linings. Tom wore the same number of layers, and it didn't feel particularly cold.

"There's a friend of yours out here," Tom said.

It was Sundance! His sorrel coat thick as a well-fed cat's now that it was winter, his intelligent eye watching me with interest.

"Just go easy. Nobody's been on him since you left."

I went easy, and Sundance responded. It felt good just to ride him.

Tom let the herd out of the corral. There was an old lead cow, and she immediately struck out, taking first place from the others. As soon as we drove them onto the prairie, the whole herd strung out behind her. The little calves fell behind and the cows went ahead, some-times bunched behind the lead cow but mostly plodding in single file. They were strung out for almost a quarter of a mile, with Tom and me riding at a walk behind them. The old lead cow seemed to know where she was going, because she hit the trail with little guidance.

Once in a while Tom lit out around the herd to turn her one way or the other but not often.

The first hour passed, but the sky grew no lighter. The sun did not come up. The ceiling hung low and gray and heavy. The old snow crackled under the hooves of horses and cattle. Windless, smoking cold breath eddied around our mouths and the heads of the stock. The little calves were silent.

About ten o'clock it began. The snow fell at first in small, dry flakes, straight down. I watched it gather on the curly, red-brown backs of the calves before me. It was beautiful. The whole world around us, locked in gray and cold, was complete and perfect for me. I was riding my maverick with the man who had broken it for me, the man I admired more than anyone else, driving cattle across the open slopes of my homeland, and I had no room nor need for any other world. When the snow stirred on the brown backs, when the flakes thickened and the wind rose, I still found not a flaw in my perfect realm.

The wind was sharp, driving the snow before it in long white strings. It came across the long slopes and frozen snow-crusted ridges with nothing to stop it. There was no growth in this region but lines of bare cottonwoods meandering along creek bottoms. The pine hills lay south, and north were only more snow-locked slopes and prairies and frozen gumbo hills.

Soon we couldn't see the lead cow. The snow heaped on the curly rumps ahead of me. I swung my rope, partly to keep my arms warm, and flicked a rump to keep it moving. What would stop us from getting lost, I wondered. We might wander forever and freeze to death, and I looked at Tom, but if any such thought came to him, he never breathed it or looked it. If we were lost, he would know what to do. He would find a creek bottom, make a lean-to of saddles, build a fire, and butcher a calf. I halfway hoped it would happen.

"Hold up, Pistol," Tom was swinging off his horse. I looked around, wondering, until I saw the little red-brown carcass stretched out in the snow. The curly flank rose and fell, rose and fell, and the soft eye was half shut. Snow had crusted on the soft caracul of the coat and the pubic hairs were a beard of ice. Tom lifted him onto his feet and held him a moment, knocking off the snow and ice, and giving him a slap, sent him ahead.

We followed. A few yards farther on, another calf lay in the snow. I jumped down and picked him up, brushing off the snow and ice and letting go with a slap. Another ten feet, a third had sprawled in a drift, stretched out upright like a merry-go-round pony. Tom got down again, and this time he didn't remount. He wrapped the reins around the saddle horn and walked ahead. As soon as I saw him wrapping the reins, I swung down, too, and dallied mine around the horn, and side by side we hiked on. The horses followed, their heads slung low and the snow instantly gathering on the saddle and along the manes where our bodies had given protection.

The old lead cow didn't stop. Somewhere a quarter or a half mile ahead, out of our sight, utterly alone in the stinging blizzard, she was breaking the trail to Wolf Creek. She led the way laterally up a long rise with the cows plodding in her hoofsteps and the little calves blindly following, with Tom and me behind. She passed over the ridge and struck a drift. The entire procession slowed noticeably, but it didn't stop. She breasted the drift as it grew deeper and deeper until it broke around her shoulders. She never halted. The cows followed through the white defile she trampled for them.

Noon came and went, and along with it my fourteen-year-old hunger pains. We had no lunch, no candy bars, no canteen of coffee, nothing. I wondered how much of the ten miles we had covered. The herd moved more and more slowly. The far side of every ridge was deep in drifts. More and more calves floundered and stopped, and we were continually lifting one out of the drift and setting him going in the beaten track. Tom laid the smallest across his empty saddle. It lay there, half dead, its flanks slowly and just perceptibly heaving under the snow which gathered swiftly over it.

The light began to fail. The gray deepened shade by shade, but the wind continued to whine past my ears, laden with snow. Every so often Tom held up his mitten and watched the snow collect on the back. "If the wind stays behind us, Pistol," he told me, "we are all right." Then he disappeared into the slot ahead, I picked up a calf lying in the trail and another sunk in the drift. I suddenly felt my aloneness and perishability against the vast, inhuman storm. I knew how easy it was to panic and rush headlong into the drifts, breasting them like great breakers until I could go no further and snuggled, exhausted as the small calf, into the folds of snow. When Tom appeared, he looked better than ever, and he said, "That old lead cow, she's quite a girl." We fell in side by side again between the last calf and the horses, and half walking, half blown, we went down the trail.

Up the rising slope, down through the drifts, along a creek bottom to the rising ground of the next ridge we plodded. It was now night. Four, six, eight o'clock I didn't know; I virtually didn't manipulate my arms and legs. They moved through the great distance of fatigue like independent mechanisms set in motion long ago. I was aware little by little that I moved more slowly, and my brain gradually came to focus on the idea that the wind had dropped. I lifted my head from the trail before me. It had stopped snowing, and the darkness was black indeed all around us.

Tom said, "There it is."

We had come to the ridge of a long slope, and across the abyss of drifts and darkness shone one small crossed square of yellow light. The shack at Wolf Creek.

There was nothing left in me for a wild, cowboy yell, but my spirits came up for a moment above the weariness. The old lead cow broke the drifts for one last time, heading downhill towards the cow camp. It lay protected somewhat under a crescent of cliff. The shack and the sheds, corrals and pens were spread out in the lee of the cliff, and the snow was not deep around them. Tom strode ahead and opened the gate for the herd to plod through. The moment they did so, the little calves bellered and the mothering up began.

In the commotion of mooing and little calf bawls, the shack door opened, a long slice of yellow light fell across the snow, and Red joined us. With a little conversation like "Howdy," "What took you so long?" "A bit snowy underfoot," Red and Tom set to work. Tom led his horse into the shed and unsaddled, and I followed him. I could hardly loosen the cinch and drag the weight of the saddle across Sundance's back. Tom measured oats for his horse, so afterwards I did. Then Tom strode to the trough and swinging an ax, broke the ice. I tottered after him and heaved the chunks out of the water, but he wouldn't let me drop them right there. I had to fling them as far as I could so that the cows wouldn't stumble on them. While we were opening the trough, Red hitched a team to a wagon, and Tom swung sacks of cottonseed cake and bales of hay into the wagon bed. I staggered after him and tried to do it, too. Then Tom climbed into the wagon and I followed, and with Red driving, we circled the pen, breaking open the sacks of cottonseed cake and snipping baling wire and emptying sacks and bales into the wagon's wake. I didn't dare stand at the edge because my legs were giving out. After an endless time the job was done, the team unhitched, and the three of us headed for the shack.

No human shelter will ever look so good to me as the cowboy shack on Wolf Creek that night. That one-room cabin with the plank floor and plank wainscoting with beaver board walls and ceiling, a window or two and the door, was lit with a gas lantern and heated to the point of suffocation by a small iron wood-burning spit-and-argue stove and a big black wood-burning cookstove. There were plank shelves for dishes and canned food and bins by the door for potatoes and onions and pegs on the wall for clothes, a table and chairs, and one large, sagging, feather-ticked double bed.

When we stepped in the door, Tom and Red began to peel. They took off their Scotch caps and mackinaws and overshoes and high-heeled boots and Levi's and shirts and wool pants until they were down to their oatmeal, button-seated, baggy-bottomed, saggy-kneed long john underwear, and there they stopped. So I shed layer after layer until I looked just like them only smaller.

Red had hauled in with us a great haunch of beef, frozen to the marrow, and flung it on the table. As soon as he was down to his long johns, he tackled it with a huge butcher knife and a meat saw and sliced a steak as thick as my forearm. Telling me to peel those spuds and stoke the fire, Red stood at the cookstove, showing us nothing but his button-seated rear view and prepared a dinner no gourmet chef will ever equal and no diner appreciate more. He fried thick slabs of home-cured bacon in a huge skillet and then heaped the potatoes I had sliced into an inch of bacon grease and cut the bacon chunks into them. He opened a great can of tomatoes and dumped them into a pan and pulled bread apart and stirred it in. He freshened the coffee pot by throwing in more grounds and pouring in more water and moving the pot to a hotter place on the stove's black surface, and then he flipped that steak into the largest skillet of all, heated smoking hot. I put a stack of bread and the bowl of home-churned butter and the canned milk and a bowl of jam on the table. When Red had everything ready, he sliced the steak onto worn tin plates, heaped the edges with fried potatoes and stewed tomatoes, and we pulled up our chairs and fell into it, hunched over it, a slice of buttered bread in one hand, smoking coffee beside our plates, saying practically nothing, just eating and eating and eating until it was all gone.

Afterwards, Tom and Red pushed back their chairs, Tom slapped his chest where his pocket should have been, looking for his cigarette makings, and his eyes met mine in a certain way so that I got up and brought his tobacco sack and washed the dishes without a word. While I washed, I listened to their laconic, understated, deadpan cowboy talk. I wanted terribly hard not to laugh out loud and be just as straight-faced as they were, but shortly I was doubled up over the dishpan, laughing so hard my stomach muscles, already weary, knotted in unbearable cramps.

I wondered where I was going to sleep since there was only one bed. Maybe Red had a bedroll somewhere. I was more than ready when Tom said, "Okay, Pistol, you get in the middle so's you don't get lost." Still in my long underwear, I crawled into the center of the ancient double bed. The coil springs groaned and creaked as Tom, over six feet and two hundred pounds, took one side, and Red, a little shorter and scrawnier, took the other. "Now, Pistol," Red said, "don't you do no thrashin'." We pulled up the feather tick, and I didn't notice anything until I heard a scratching.

When I opened my eyes, I found the cabin flooded with blinding sun, and I saw Tom in his long johns standing at the window, scraping away the frost with his pocketknife. Red swung out of bed and leaned over his shoulder. The cabin was icy.

"It fell some," Red said.

"You read it and tell me," Tom stepping aside.

"I read sixty-three below."

"That's what I read."

I read the thermometer myself. There was no mistake. The mercury had fallen to sixty-three below.

We stoked the fires and dressed in the numerous layers, pulling scarves around our mouths and noses until only the eyes showed, and went out. The routine care was the same as the first night. We moved very slowly to avoid deep breathing. The air was like a knife blade in my lungs, and my nostrils seemed to stick together after each inhalation.

When we finished, Red prepared another monumental meal. This time he scraped away a layer of lard in a crock and extracted pork sausage patties, and he fried them along with another heaping skillet of potatoes and stacks of wheat cakes, hot Mapleine syrup, and coffee.

At breakfast Tom said that we wouldn't be going back that day. We'd just have to wait till the cold broke. I didn't care if it never did.

The days went by, and the cow camp remained locked in deep cold. We fed and watered the stock several times each day. Tom checked each animal daily and doctored those that needed it. Red made us boots of newspaper that fitted inside the overshoes, and we wore these instead of leather boots for warmth. We put on tin pants, lined canvas trousers, when we went out, and we moved slowly and never stayed long. When they weren't worn, the tin pants still looked inhabited, hanging in a row against the wall. In between I listened to Red and Tom making cowboy talk, hilarious tales of past roundups and drives and trips to town and mutual acquaintances, that broke me up over the dishpan or the cards or the checkerboard. The airtight shack grew strong with wood fires and leather and horse clothes and men in long underwear. The dashes to the outhouse were the fastest of my career. As Red said, all the constipated people in Montana had to be buried in a sitting position that year, just plumb froze stiff. My spirits sank on the morning I awoke in my niche in the feather bed to find the weather noticeably warmer.

Tom and I rode side by side on the trail home. It was the same one the old lead cow had broken. We trotted most of the way in the brilliant sun and arrived at Tom's place just after noon. Sam's Model A was sitting in the yard. I asked Sam what day it was, and it was past

New Year's. Christmas was over. I had been gone two weeks with no word to anyone, and in a frozen cow camp eighty miles from home, which was in the middle of nowhere, anyway, I had had the time of my life.

Sam took me into town that afternoon and let me off in front of our ample old house. My mother was hurt and lifted her chin and cried a little that I hadn't been there for Christmas. My father and Conrad bawled me out for wounding my mother — didn't I have any consideration for others — but later Conrad asked me how it was out there, and I said diffidently, "A bit snowy underfoot," the way, I hoped, that Tom had said it.

No Meanness
to Remember

8

I had learned finally and for all, I told myself, not to talk about what mattered to me. I didn't even tell Richie much about the cow camp at Wolf Creek, and I waited for the urge to tell to drift on. But it didn't. It grew more pressing and worried me that I'd start blabbing in front of Conrad. One afternoon after school I got to the corner right behind Allison Mitchell, and she smiled and said, "Were you out at Sam's over Christmas?" and I said, "I was," and she said, "I went out to the ranch with Daddy. Were you caught in the blizzard, too?" Then I told her the whole story, as we walked between the dikes of snow, and she listened and laughed. I felt very good, relieved like a pop bottle letting out its fizz, and I liked her even better than I had. She didn't flirt, and she talked about the ranch life around Pumpkin Creek, what we both knew and liked best.

The days lengthened as the curve of the year rose, and the sun grew more brilliant on the plains of snow. The day after a late March storm left water-heavy drifts too bright to look at, Mr. Burbank brought *Giants in the Earth* to a close. Per Hansa died in a blizzard. Tears streamed down Allison's face. My own lips trembled. We filed from the classroom not looking at each other. In that night's paper Hack Davis's father reported just such a death on a ranch close by.

Maybe it came from my self-imposed silence, my growing restlessness at home. It was partly that, and partly from the unceasing bickering between my father and Conrad. Every night something put them crossways of each other. Conrad usually came out winning the argument for no particular reason that I could see, but my father always hit a place where he stopped fighting back. This bothered me as much as anything, although more than half the time I figured Conrad was right. The arguments began halfway through dessert, and I found myself reluctant to eat the first spoonful. Conrad, sharp-nosed and squint-eyed, would turn up the first card, or my father, still spruce, he called it, in his white shirt with the starched detachable collar and his tie and pinch-waist double-breasted suit coat, would open provocatively.

Bewilderment, distress clouded and distorted my mother's face. She protested; she covered her face with her hands; and finally she threw down her napkin and left the kitchen.

With my fists in the soapsuds I stared into the black window and wished with all my guts to be away from here. Let it blow. Freeze. Dry up. I'd take my chances with Tom and Sam, no matter what happened. The sooner I got back out there and away from this misery wouldn't be too soon for me.

I began to look for Sam's Model A every day as spring advanced. I changed my route from school to the drugstore to go past the feedstore where he would go when he came into town. I watched for him on Main Street, in front of the saddlery, on the side street by the Marshall House or the Laurel. I watched, waiting, until one suddenly warm April afternoon I saw the little coupe standing in front of the feedstore. Sam must be there, and as I looked around for him, the great barn door slid open and he stepped out.

I grinned irrepressibly.

"Well, Pistol," he said, "I've been thinking about you." He jumped to the ground from the raised loading dock, and we grinned at each other, shaking hands. "You're coming out pretty soon."

It was not quite a question, not quite a statement, and I nodded happily.

"I sure am," I said, "if you want me."

"No other horse wrangler's ridden in lately," he said, lifting his hat and rumpling his crinkly gray hair. "It may be another dry one, Pistol."

Another drought summer, possibly more severe than the preceding years, was already the topic of conversation in town. Men at the pens, on the streets, in the shops and offices murmured, it doesn't look too good. They watched the weather from the corners of their eyes as if to look at it straight would bring bad luck. But I didn't realize how serious conditions were until I rode in Sam's Model A across the prairies again.

The prairie had not greened up. In the little **damp** places where water collected from rain or a hidden spring, the tiny prairie lilies had not appeared. There was no surface water. The grasses were stunted, brown as August. Among the sage and cholla the magpies flashed black and white against the sand-brown, unrelieved by any mitigating green.

But what did it matter? I was going back, wasn't I? Sam's Model A sped down the last hill. I watched the leaves of the great cottonwoods around the main ranch shiver first silver and then dark in the wind.

On the porch Mrs. Gallagher turned from banging the triangle and cried out, "Billy's here!" bringing Lacey to the screen door, smiling and looking at me with more interest than last year. Now the men were coming up the lane from the corrals and the bunkhouse, Texas Diller limping a little and Fonse walking swiftly past him, paying no attention, but Red drew up and was saying something, then Roscoe with the milk pails, and Seth setting his own pace and beside him Tom, tall and big and walking so lightly that it seemed he carried all his weight in his shoulders.

When they reached me, they grinned and said, "Howdy, Pistol," "How's everything?" "School out? Hope it didn't hurt you none," and they gripped my hand in their roughened brown paws and clapped me on the shoulder.

Taking turns at the washbasin, as they mopped their faces and tossed the water into the yard, they questioned me on this and that and kidded me, laughing, with Tom standing by, grinning, passing a wink to me, his eyes crinkled up, and I knew I was home.

98

The screen door creaked and slammed as we went into the great kitchen to find our places beside the long oilcloth-covered table already steaming with serving dishes. Waiting a split second to see if my last year's seat had been taken by someone else, which it hadn't, I sat down across from Tom, and I looked down the table to make sure that the extra empty place was set and waiting for any drifting stranger who might ride in, which it was. Spoons clinked against crockery, forks clattered, bony shoulders in faded work shirts hunched forward, a sun-blackened hand holding a chunk of white bread, few words were exchanged until the serving bowls had been emptied and filled two times and the coffee was going around.

"Anybody seen Sundance?" I asked. In my mind I saw him, his long, uncut sorrel-red mane which swept below his neck and the long, untrimmed sorrel-red tail which brushed the ground, and the sunlight playing on his burnished coat.

"I brought him in the other day," Tom said, and then I noticed the stir of interest among the other riders, their faces turning towards me, their eyes flickering.

"He hasn't been rid since you was out Christmas," Red said. "He's waitin' for you, Pistol."

Texas Diller drawled, "We knowed you'd want to shake him down yourself."

An icy chill squeezed my stomach. Since the winter drive I had ridden nothing more fractious than a school-room desk, and I was out of practice. Any horse that had gone unridden had to have the kinks taken out of him. I knew that Sundance gentled only last year could have returned to his original wildness. But he was assigned to me, and I had to ride him. I knew what was coming with dead certainty, and my heart sank. At least he had been in the corral a few days. Tom had seen to that.

I looked down the table. All the faces were alive and watching me. With his eye on me, Fonse rolled a cigarette, his lank straight hair swinging down over his forehead. Texas Diller held his coffee cup to his mouth and watched me over the rim as he sucked off long swallows the way you drink standing with your seat close to a fire on a very cold night. Old Seth McCollum looked straight at me, his watery red-veined eyes in questioning appraisal. To heck with them, Tom would help me. I turned back to Tom and searched his face for reassurance, but he wasn't even looking at me. Stirring his mudbrown coffee he gazed far away.

Lonesomeness filled me. My first feeling of welcome, the generosity of the long table with its extra place set for a stranger, disappeared in the pit of my stomach. Tomorrow morning I had to ride Sundance gone wild and make a damn public fool of myself for all those punchers' entertainment. I sighed as I crawled into bed in the spare room and looked at the round flat face of the Big Ben clock with the bicycle bell on top and listened to its marching tick-tick, tick-tick.

Sleep refused to creep over me, and I stared at the dim wallpaper. I saw myself in the round corral face-to-face with Sundance gone wild. How was I going to saddle him, ride him? How was I even going to catch him? I turned back to the ticking clock. I went over everything I had learned from Tom as he gentled Sundance the summer before. Tom had worked slow and easy, giving the young horse time to get used to every step. All the while from the corral fence Red gave him the benefit of his opinion, that the way to break a horse was to break him, snub him and saddle him and ride him out until he knew who was boss, and the others had agreed with him, but Tom ignored them and gentled Sundance and had shown me how to do it, and I could see him still working in the corral and telling me, "If you want a good horse, don't give him no reason to fear you. Don't give him no meanness to remember."

In the end Sundance was gentled and not broken and was a horse of great beauty, spirit and intelligence, but Tom's way was difficult. It took time and endless patience, and, what made my stomach sink now, great skill. I stared at the dark ceiling above the bed.

First, I had to catch Sundance in the corral. I could rope him, or, Tom's way, walk up to him and slip the hackamore over his head, but I could see myself working all morning trying to get close enough to use a hackamore, and the prospect of the cowboy razzing I'd get almost sickened me. I tossed and sighed. I had to rope him, something Tom had done only at the very first, but now roping was the only way. Tom wouldn't like it. I would disappoint Tom, the man I wanted to resemble exactly. Well, it couldn't be helped. Tom wouldn't like it, but he wouldn't say anything.

Then, I had to saddle him. I stared at the lilacs in the wallpaper. If he showed signs of making trouble, I could snub him fast to the post in the middle of the corral. Then when I had him saddled and I let him loose, then I had to mount him and ride him. The emptiness in my stomach came close to making me sick, and I kept swallowing too sweet saliva again and again as I stared into the broad, flat face of the clock.

That morning I tried not to walk too slowly down the lane to the horse barn and corrals. The ground fell away a little so that I had a full view of the pens, and I could see that all the punchers were already there. Red and Texas Diller stood talking together, and nearby Fonse worked on something with Seth McCollum. I looked everywhere anxiously for Tom, but he wasn't in sight. I had almost reached the corral when he came out of the pen, leading his favorite little horse, and he grinned slightly at me and said, "Mornin', Pistol," and as he passed me, he handed me his soft and worn old hackamore.

Then I knew what I had to do. The ribbing, the humiliation, I had to take them. Now I had to take on Sundance as Tom had taught me. I tucked the rope into my back pocket and climbed the corral fence.

Immediately the hats and heads and eyes strung out along the top rail.

The horses bunched and raced to the opposite side of the round corral. The hooves pounded, manes and tails swept away, heads tossed as they kept a wary eye on me. I moved toward them, seeing in the middle of the bunch the rusty pumpkin color of my horse shining in the sun. I moved in, cutting them one by one to left and right until Sundance stood alone against the rails.

Had he forgotten everything? He had his nose to the fence and his rump toward me, just what Tom had taught him not to do, and when I spoke to him, he did not turn at the sound of my voice. He looked ready to explode. I spoke to him again. He gave his head a long shuddering shake. Whispering to him, I moved forward step by step. Was there a change in that bulging eye? "Sundance, baby, you're looking good," I said, and then, suddenly, I could hardly believe it, he turned toward me. He quivered all over. I stopped still and whispered to him. I held out my empty hand. He snuffed it and tossed his head. Moving in inch by inch, I touched his velvet nose and hard flat cheeks, and he stood still listening to my voice and I waited until his quivering stopped and slipped on the old soft hackamore. I rubbed all around his nose and neck where the rope settled, and as I rubbed, I glanced sidelong at the top rail to see all the heads and hats and eyes looking the other way and beyond them Tom busy saddling his horse, bending over and straightening, and when he straightened, he scanned the corral before he bent to the cinch again.

I could have laughed out loud, but instead I pressed my teeth together and tried not to smile.

Very slowly, talking and clucking to him all the time, I led Sundance to the corral gate and in a burst of bravado I decided to saddle him outside the fence, and then if he bucked all over, well, let him buck and I'd try to hold on until we got out of sight. I opened the gate and led him through, and passing between the men and Tom, Tom held out the currycomb for me, grinning just a little.

While I brushed and curried the rough winter coat, I worked carefully so that I didn't give Sundance any reason to fear me. I showed him the blanket before throwing it over his back and waited until he got used to it, and I hooked one stirrup over the horn and tucked the latigo through its buckle so that no loose end would flap and frighten him as the unaccustomed weight of the saddle suddenly settled down on his back. I pulled up the cinch carefully. Whatever happened next, I didn't want it to come loose. Then I led Sundance into the open, took a short and tight hold on the left-hand rein,

turning his head toward me, and twisted the left stirrup
forward to give my knee pressure against his shoulder.
His brown eye bulged and rolled. I gripped reins and
mane and saddlehorn, gave a little push-off shove with
my right foot, and swung into the saddle. Whiffing and
snorting, Sundance pranced sideways across the yard,
tossed his head hard against the rein, but I held him
high and whispered to him and wanted to laugh out
loud, and I turned him around and trotted him up and
down, and the row of deadpan faces and hats over the
eyes turned the other way, and I heard Tom say, "You
boys goin' to ride or you goin' to stand there all day?"

"Just as soon ride," Texas Diller drawled. "Nothin'
much goin' on around here."

Up and down, across and back again, I trotted and
turned the little horse until I could feel him relax and
fall in with me so that I relaxed and loosened my short
grip on the reins. Now I could feel us moving together,
and I could no longer hold back a joyous ear to ear grin.
Oh, that beautiful little horse, his sorrel mane shining
and his earth-length sorrel tail sweeping behind him!
That magnificent horse, he had forgotten nothing. And
I grinned with joy, neither had I. I could do it. I not
only could do it, I had done it. I had done it! And not
simply done it, I had done it in the best and most difficult way. I had learned how, I knew how, and I had
done it.

When the cowboys had mounted and we bunched up
riding away from the corrals, Tom came up beside me,
his eyes squinted against the sun and his half-smiling
lips clamped on his little dead crimped roll-your-own
cigarette, and as he passed, he said to me, "He's lookin'
pretty good for a kid horse."

The Mitchell Place

9

From that moment the rhythm of ranch life caught me up. I knew my work much better and began to fill in the chinks with practice, as Tom said. We rode circle and swept the hills and prairies clean of stock and branded in the open around the cottonwood fires. We worked the odd jobs, riding fence and doctoring and making repairs and doing chores.

Each day I woke up limp and heavy and warm and lay there not thinking yet. Then I was sitting on the edge of the bed pulling on my boots, and I went through the kitchen which was empty still and let the screen door bang behind me. I poured some water into the chipped enamel basin by the door and splashed it, wonderfully cold, over my face and set my dirty hat down on my head and after stopping by the outhouse started out for the corrals. Below me I saw the whole spread of pens and barns and lean-to's silent and still and barely touched by the morning sun, and above them, protect-

ing them, the shoulder of hill buff color and scattered
with wind-twisted pine. I aimed a rock at a magpie
where he pecked in some manure and missed him a mile
which I intended, anyway, but throwing, I could feel
my muscles hardening and I was ready to burst, just
feeling good. The mistakes I made yesterday which had
me squirming didn't seem so bad anymore. In the smells
of dung and dust, hemp and leather and horseflesh I
saddled up, and I rode out onto the prairie to wrangle
the remuda again this morning, which I did so that the
hands could ride to mend fences and doctor cattle and
drive them to more plentiful grass so that they would be
beefed out by time for the fall drive so that they could
be sold and shipped from the stock pens in my home
town to bring in cash for supplies and breeding stock
and cowhands' and wranglers' pay, making the whole
known world go round. There was nobody to tell me I
was too young, I didn't know enough, or I didn't know
the right things. I knew I had a place, and I knew what
to do, at least how to start doing it, the way I knew how
to breathe, so that this day, each day, its rhythm and
deepest meaning were known without asking.

Always there was an undercurrent of worry about
range conditions. In spite of winter losses Sam still ran a
large herd, and he had Seth McCollum drive some cattle
early up to the summer range. Things were bad and
getting worse but I forget all about them. Mrs. Gallagher
said one night, "There's a letter for you, Billy." I didn't
recognize the writing on the blue envelope, and inside it
didn't say much, only, "I'd love to see you, Allison."

"D'ya think the female of the species takes an interest
in Pistol?" Texas asked the supper table.

"What makes you think so?" I said.

"A man always writes his love letters on a brown paper bag," Texas said, "and he says romantic things like kin you cook and keep house good. Now the female is always decoratin' the necessities, curtains and blue writin' paper and what not."

"If you're goin' courtin'," Fonse said, "Red can give you the particulars. He's been courtin' the Widow Garrison for years."

"Git off me," Red growled. "Driscoll's the one. One time he knew every woman in eastern Montana, but they weren't good enough or bad enough for him, I don't know which."

They had eyes like eagles. I had better come out with it, and I asked Sam if he needed me after dinner, because if he didn't I'd ride over to the Mitchell place.

Tom smiled and winked at me. "Not bad for a start," he said.

"You can borrow my tuxedo, Pistol," Fonse said. "You'll be gettin' there about their dinnertime."

"Don't listen to them, Billy," said Mrs. Gallagher. "You look real handsome."

The Mitchell's main house lay close to the road, protected on one side by a windbreak of pine and poplar and silvery Russian olive. The drive curved close to the front door. I tied Sundance in the windbreak, wondering if it was the front door like in town or the kitchen like a working ranch. I had never been there, and I began to question my nerve, thinking about which door. Few people had been inside the Mitchell place. Mr. Mitchell always rode on the big roundups and drives and carried a lot of weight with the cattlemen's association. Sam called him Terence, but his own riders, even his foreman, called him Mr. Mitchell. Behind his back other cowboys called him ole Mitchell and ole horse blanket because of his jacket. To his face they called him no name at all. I decided to try it like a front door first and think of something else later. There was a small brass handle which I twisted, and a bell jingled on the other side. Then, beyond the door I heard movement, and the door opened. It was Mr. Mitchell's man, Jeffrey, in a white coat. I stared at the coat and couldn't say anything.

"She is at dinner," Jeffrey said, looking me over. I stared at him. I twisted my hat. I swallowed.

"It's Billy Catlett! Oh, hi!"

Jeffrey stepped back for Allison. "Come in! We're just having coffee in the living room. Did you get my letter? I was hoping you were out here again." Allison had her hair divided in two, each hank wrapped in those crazy squaw ribbons, and no more dressed up than beaded white moccasions and a clean white shirt. Her Levi's showed as much soil as any cowboy's. She took my hand in her warm, slim fingers, and led me into the living room.

Mr. Mitchell, dressed in his horse blanket tweed jacket, rose and greeted me, shaking hands, and Allison said, "Mother, may I present Billy Catlett?" Seated on the couch, Mrs. Mitchell smiled and held out her hand, not her shaking hand, and I wondered what I should do with it — kiss it maybe? — but she pressed my hand and withdrew hers before I had to decide, and I almost forgot to say anything because she looked so much like Allison, the same bony nose and cheekbones and pleasant brown eyes and welcoming smile, the thick gray braids wound around her head.

"Please sit down, my dear. Another cup, Jeffrey,

please." Her dress came to the floor. So it was true. At the Mitchell place one woman dressed for dinner. She poured black coffee from a silver pot into tiny gold-rimmed cups.

"What did Sam say about the stockmen's meeting the other night?" Mr. Mitchell asked.

"He said he thought they had the right idea."

"Oh, Daddy, can't we talk about something else?"

"Young Bill's as interested as I am, Allison. So is your mother."

"Daddy thinks they had the wrong idea." Allison laughed gaily.

"I meant about the feed per head. That's what Sam thought was the right idea."

"That is exactly what I question."

I swallowed. I didn't see how it could be questioned, but I didn't want to get in an argument with her father right off. For a second I watched Jeffrey clearing the three places in the dining room beyond — the hands must eat somewhere else — and wished for a shot of tin cow in my black and bitter coffee.

"But the people from the agricultural station said that grass was sufficient without feeding hay if you add one pound of cottonseed cake every day. And I guess they can prove it."

"Sufficient for what? The agricultural station is concerned with survival. All right, I grant you, it's pressing, but we must think beyond today. We must ask ourselves, are we running the best breed of cattle for the range? How can we get more beef, better beef in the shortest time for the least investment? There is considerable research going on in this vein back East, in Iowa and various places, in England and Scotland. I said as much the other night, but as soon as the East is mentioned, you know what happens. Every rancher thinks of the scoundrel who holds his mortgage, and suspicion carries the day."

"There's no use thinking beyond today, if you're not going to be here," I said.

"Billy has a very good point, Terence." Smiling, Mrs. Mitchell filled the cups again.

"The agricultural people are thinking about what is here now, Daddy."

"I am not unappreciative of that, Allison, but breeding may be the decisive factor."

I nearly blew the coffee out of my cup. Nobody talked about breeding in front of women. I flushed to the roots of my hair.

"If we can breed a strain that can take range conditions the way the present stock does . . ." I looked around. No one was the least disturbed. ". . . and resists disease and fattens on fewer acres, then we will have a range stock par excellence, don't you agree?"

I nodded. I didn't dare ask, but how? Mr. Mitchell would tell me.

"Allison, has young Bill seen Domino?"

"Billy just got here, Daddy."

"Take him down to the corrals and show him Domino. I have a little research of my own going. Let me know what you think of it."

I thanked Mrs. Mitchell for the coffee, and she smiled and held out her squeezing hand and said, "Do come again, my dear. Allison is quite lonely out here this year."

It was a relief to get away. Not that they were unfriendly or the room inhospitable. The furniture was covered in unbleached muslin, and the draperies at the long windows were unbleached muslin, what the poorest ranch wife made herself from empty hundred-pound flour sacks. With the Navajo rugs and the hide of a gigantic grizzly bear with a fanged head the size of a tub on the floor, it was like other ranches. Still there was something more to it which maybe the silver pot and the gold-rimmed cups and the talk added.

Lightning suddenly clawed the western sky.

"Heat lightning!" we exclaimed together. It was more to be feared than an electrical storm. In the dry grass the tiniest spark could catch fire and the wind would sweep it through the grass for miles with no rain to check its advance.

A screen door slammed. Cowboys ran out of the bunkhouse and pulled up, shading their eyes to the west. We all stood tense and alert and scanned the horizon for the telling curl of smoke. After a few minutes nothing appeared, and I heard one man say, "And I had a pair of aces." They disappeared again.

"The heat lightning makes Domino awfully restless," Allison said.

In the dusk of the barn the odors of sweet hay, oats, dust, manure freshly dropped, horse flesh assailed me with marvelous familiarity. Walking down the center aisle, I saw that a horse occupied each stall, the first time I had seen such practice on the range. These horses were brushed and clean and their hides showed no nicks from barbed wire or cactus or mean brood mares.

At the last stall Allison climbed on the lowest plank. I followed her and looked. A gigantic black bull pawed the ground and snuffled nervously.

"That's Domino," Allison said.

After a stunned moment I said, "That's quite an animal." I had never seen his equal. His great black nose was wet and running and his eyes almost started from his heavy head. His back was enormous and flat and lustrously black, and his rear end was staggering. I remembered a cattle auctioneer I had heard once hollering, "Look at his rear end, folks, this bull's got lots of bull." I was horribly embarrassed.

"Where'd you get him?"

"Daddy had him sent from Scotland. He's a blooded Aberdeen Angus bull. Daddy wants to see if Angus do better than range critters."

"Boy, he must have made a stir in town when he came in. I'm surprised I didn't hear about it."

"Oh, he didn't come on the train. He came in a special truck all the way from New York, just like a racehorse. The sides were padded with quilts and he had special food and the driver was insured by Lloyd's of London. The railroad wouldn't touch him."

"Do you have blooded brood cows, too? Black ones?"

"They're coming, and that's the trouble, I guess. Daddy's worried they won't get here for this year's breeding."

"What's he going to do? Scotland isn't like this. How will they stand it at forty below with the wind coming down from the North Pole? They may not even know what a cactus is and take a bite. Look at his legs, Allison, look how short they are. How is he going to get through the brush and rock? A critter has to range far and wide to get enough feed in grassland, and he has to be able to take care of himself, resist disease and all that. I don't see how your dad . . ."

"Daddy thinks they may fatten without roaming so far. He says he's going to use supplementary feed all year round."

"But that's expensive. Range cattle already are tough and resistant, and if you add cottonseed cake the way the agricultural station says, why go to all the bother. I mean . . ."

"Daddy's experimenting. It's worth trying. I quite agree with that."

"Yeah, sure, I do, too, but . . ."

Lightning cracked again. We ran outside and scanned the horizon where it had raked the sky. No sign of fire.

"I guess I'd better head back," I said.

We walked side by side up the lane toward the house. When we were hidden in the shade under a cottonwood, Allison suddenly took my hand and squeezed it and smiled her warmest smile and said, "I hope you'll come back."

I squeezed back and caught her arm under mine, pulling her close to me. "I'd sure like to," I said.

She pulled away and brushed her sleeve, straightening it and laughing.

She watched as I checked the cinch and saddle on Sundance and walked him away from the hitching rack.

"That's a beautiful horse," she said.

"This time last year," I said, "he was running wild. He was a maverick."

"Oh, I remember him. He used to lead the wild horses. We used to see him on the ridges."

Sundance skittered spiritedly as I swung on, and I set my hat and said, "I'll be back," with a grin and urged him into a fast trot so that his broomtail streamed out behind him. From the road I waved, but she had turned toward the house and was walking slowly away, looking down.

For a few minutes I kept the pace, as if I had struck it from urgency, but when we settled into the steady trot homeward, I felt my exhilaration sweep on in some other kind of necessity. I wasn't going to tell Red and Fonse or anybody, maybe Tom later, about the Mitchell place; I intended to think of something suitably laconic to say because I knew they'd be eaten up with curiosity; but now I was busting. When I told them about that bull, their mouths would drop to their boot tops. And if they knew I had heard it from a girl, but I would never tell them that. You never mentioned such things in front of women; you never called a bull a bull; you said animal; and all those hands would wonder what kind of a girl she was to wear pants and talk about such things. It was a funny conversation to have with a girl, I thought so, too, although it hadn't seemed funny at the time, except for the horrible moment when I knew we were looking at the same thing. The conversation had come as naturally as talking with another boy, only Allison was not a boy. A girl you could treat like a woman and talk with like a man, not flirt all the time with the tossing sausage curls, was a very easy girl to be around. Maybe I could get her to undo those squaw braids. The lightning struck again, clawing the edge of the night sky.

I began to ride every few days over to the Mitchell place. We did some kissing in the tack room, surrounded by the pungent smell of leather, where the saddles sat on sawhorses and the bridles hung on hooks and the martingales, latigoes and spare parts made an array like a saddle shop.

"Billy," Allison whispered, "you'd better not come so often."

"I thought you liked me."

She threw me a dark look. "I like you a lot. This is Mum's old sidesaddle," and she stroked it and dusted it. The seat was upholstered in soft leather tooled like embroidery.

"What's wrong then?"

"It's Daddy. Daddy's funny."

"Doesn't he want anybody liking you?"

"I don't know, but early this summer he fired a new rider for hanging around all the time. He said he didn't do his work, but I couldn't see that he didn't. He was awfully old, maybe twenty-six even, and he kept making jokes about fifteen was a good time to get married, because at sixteen you started to decay and how he had a place up in the hills but he needed a woman to take the lonesomeness off it. Well, after two weeks of hanging around, Daddy fired him."

"Maybe he couldn't take the jokes," I said, but some nervousness came over me. Mr. Mitchell was a formidable father.

"Well, then, how about every third night after this?"

"Oh, swell, Billy," she whispered, and leaning across the sidesaddle, she kissed me.

But it was easier said than obeyed. I carved *A*'s in lonely fence posts, a slash the first day, a slash the second, on the third the crossbar, and I was off. When I arrived, I talked for a while over the coffee and kept a weather eye on Mr. Mitchell. He seemed entirely agreeable, and he liked to talk, giving me his theories on genetics, British politics, the uses of grasslands, and world empire. He didn't like agreement; he wanted to overwhelm you with his argument, which he proceeded to do until Mrs. Mitchell said, "Terence, these young people don't want to sit here all evening. You may be excused, dears." With Mrs. Mitchell on my side, I lost my caution. Instinctive wariness sent no messages, and I began to ride over every other evening, then every night until I had to see her so urgently that I broke away in midafternoon and set out.

She was leading her strawberry roan mare from the barn when I saw her, and I rode down upon her, my heart hammering.

"I was just thinking about you," she said. "How did you get off at this time of day?"

"I guess I got your thought. Something told me to come and see you."

She laughed. "You haven't come the other times I've thought of you."

I stood beside her. "I had to see you, for my own reasons."

"And I think about you all the time, anyway."

We rode that day to the long meadow of native hay which followed the creek through the Mitchell place. At the barbed wire gate I dismounted and opened it, and helped Allison down and side by side we walked through the rolling field. I took her hand. "Grass is the most beautiful thing I know of."

"I love it," she said, our shoulders brushing.

Hot sun, sweet grass, sweet-smelling hair, suddenly she put out her foot and tripped me and ran off, laughing.

"All right," I said, "now you're going to get it."

I sprinted after her, and when she turned and flashed a smile at me over her shoulder, I let go with a flying tackle and downed her in the grass. We rolled over and over, laughing, and she tried to tickle me and I tickled her back until she begged for mercy and brushing my hand over her breasts, I straightened her shirt.

Suddenly serious, she sat up. I lay on my back and watched her. She looked like a ten-year-old again.

"I don't want to do that," she said.

"Scared?" I said.

She nodded. One blue ribbon had fallen from a hank of hair, and now one side hung loose over her shoulder, swinging as she nodded.

"Me, too, kind of," I said.

"My ribbon's fallen off. Do you see my ribbon?" Her hands parted the grass, and she searched around her.

I shook my head. I felt horrible; I wanted to put my arms around her and comfort her and tell her I wouldn't ever try anything she didn't like.

"You've taken my ribbon," she said, trying to roll me aside. I made deadweight and didn't move. Suddenly I knew with absolute certainty that she would be back for more of what she didn't want and was afraid of. I lay motionless, watching her.

"You've hidden it," she said, leaning over me and searching through the grass on the other side. "I think you're mean." She brushed my chest carefully with just the touch of her shirt and took my shoulders in her hands and pretended to pull me up. I reached up and loosened the other ribbon. "What's the matter with your hair like that?" I held her face in my hands. "I don't know," she whispered. When I pulled her mouth

117

down to mine, her hair swung forward and hid our faces like dark brown curtains.

That day I raced away. I put Sundance to a full gallop for a mile. I pulled him up short. I zigzagged back and forth across the road in a parade step. I sang at the top of my voice. Turning into Sam's road, I raised a plume of dust you could see for five miles until I came down the hill in full sight of the open porch. There they lounged. Tom smoking, his cupped hand over his mouth. Red against a post. Texas seated on the edge. Fonse combing his hair, watching me.

"Hurry up, Mrs. Gallagher's waiting," Sam yelled.

Was it that late? Tying Sundance to the hitching rack, I knew, oh, God, I was going to get it. Then out of my dust came a little truck, driving too fast downhill toward the house. The Mitchell pickup! My stomach hit my throat. My God! Mr. Mitchell was chasing me!

I plunged my shaking hands into the washbasin and watched through the mottled mirror.

The little pickup skidded to a halt. The door opened, and Mr. Mitchell's man, Jeffrey, stepped out.

Sam left the porch and went toward him, saying, "Howdy, Jeffrey," in a vaguely questioning tone.

"Mr. Tolliver, sir," Jeffrey said as they met, "Mr. Mitchell asked me to inform you. Long Prairie is on fire."

The men stirred like a wind passing over them.

"Mr. Mitchell asks if you can spare a hand or two . . ."

"How many do they need?" Sam said.

Jeffrey hesitated, and then he said, "Mr. Mitchell says, sir, all you can spare."

Prairie Fire

10

The heat lightning had touched down. Somewhere unseen in the grass of the summer range it had struck the crumbling dry stubble, perhaps during the night when no one could detect the little curl of smoke and no rider saw it until he rode from camp in the morning. Then he hightailed it to the nearest ranch to give the word. The alarm had spread from there, carried from one ranch to the next until it reached Sam's place passed on by Mr. Mitchell's man.

Before Jeffrey had turned the truck around in the yard, Sam consulted the men at the table. "Pistol, bring the horses in right away," he said. "You take over, Tom, and I'll go on ahead in the Model A. We'll put everything we can in there."

"I'll get the dinner right on," said Mrs. Gallagher. "You can't set out on empty stomachs. You don't know when you'll see food next."

The remuda had not had time to wander far, and I

brought them right in. Already every shovel and ax and gunny sack and an old oil drum had been loaded into the rumble seat of the Model A coupe. As soon as the men saddled their freshest horses, we set out at a rapid trot, fast but paced, and bunched together as if we were setting out to ride circle. Driving cattle it took us a day to reach the summer grazing land in the national forest. How long it would take us now I didn't know. Soon it would be night, and the rendezvous place Jeffrey had specified lay well beyond the last ranch, Allie Bassett's, and deep in the summer range. For a time we rode in silence.

"I'll bet it's them Indians," Texas said. "They gone and set a fire to get paid for fightin' it."

Red cursed prolifically. "I'll lynch 'em, every one," he said.

"White man heap smart," Tom said. "They have some cattle up there, too."

Everyone grazed in common on the summer range. It was government land, and each rancher secured a permit to graze so many head. When the grass on the home ranch gave out toward the middle of summer, each rancher drove all the cattle his permit allowed to the higher, less arid regions of the national forest. Some of Sam's herd were up there now with Seth McCollum, and the rest of us expected to drive what remained in a few days. Whether we did would depend now on the fire.

Passing a barbed wire gate, Dominic Arlo joined us.

"Do you know when it started?" Tom asked.

"Last night," Dominic said. "One of the rangers stopped by my place to use the telephone."

"Then Long Prairie's pretty much burned out."

Dominic made a gesture of rising smoke. In silence we rode on.

In the twilight we came abreast of a small ranch house in a bare yard bordered by a rickety picket fence. As we passed, a young woman and a child came out of the house and stood watching us, the woman with her hands twisted in her apron. Red lifted his hat and said, "Evenin', ma'm," and she nodded. The child waved in delight with his whole arm. Her man had already gone. It was a meager, marginal place with probably no more than a hundred head. If they lost their range, they lost everything. I hurried to catch up.

As night closed in, we left the road and cut across country. Now we rode through the scattered pine and spruce and juniper. I could smell their fragrance and see their shapes against the sky. Other men joined us, sometimes with a greeting, sometimes saying nothing at all so that I looked up in surprise to find another dark, unrecognizable figure in our company.

A few yards after we went through a fence where the barbed wire had been hastily cut away, Tom said, "Hold it a minute, boys." We pulled up listening. "I think they're comin' that way," Tom said. We moved aside with Tom leading when I heard a faint whistle, then a shout, the heavy beat of hooves coming louder, nearer, the troubled mooing, the whine and crack of ropes being swung and brought down, more hoarse calls, and a herd pounded by us. Among the riders I picked out Seth McCollum.

Tom called out to him, and he pulled aside. They spoke, but I couldn't hear, we were too strung out now. Seth moved on, and we picked up our pace, pushing even a little faster.

Towards midnight I sniffed the scent of wood smoke, pine smoke, borne toward me on the steady wind. Beyond the next ridge rose the white glow of Coleman lanterns, growing brighter as we came near. We had reached the rendezvous.

We threaded our way through the parked cars and ranch trucks and trucks which bore the forest service emblem and found makeshift hitching racks nailed quickly between the trees to tie our horses. Around us the activity continued without pause. Cursing and shouting, two men hitched a fresno to a team, and another harnessed a hand slip. The handles of the heart-shaped spades were stacked like wigwams of guns in some long ago frontier fort. Axes for hewing and axes for grubbing were laid out in orderly rows on the ground. Gunny sacks were stacked high, and empty oil drums were loaded into the truck beds. I saw Sam's Model A, but he was nowhere in sight.

Who was giving orders I couldn't tell, but men jumped into the backs of trucks and roared away and others in gangs left the holding area walking fast. Before I knew it, someone pressed a spade into my hand and yelled, "Come on," and I followed, jumping into the back of a forest service pickup which immediately rattled off into the night. Where we were going I didn't know, but closer to the fire. The wood smoke with its reminder of campfire and winter nights at home was no longer pleasant, no longer a smell even, but a thickness like a cloud in my lungs. When the truck stopped, the gang jumped out and I jumped with them, climbing the next ridge and scrambling down, trying to see the rocks and brush before I ran into them, through the trees and out into the open. One by one the men dropped off and

I was told to dig a furrow two feet wide and throw the debris on the fire side, toward the wind, and keep at it, and the rest of the gang disappeared into the dark and I was alone in the smoke-thick cavern of night.

I began to dig. The soil was thin and stony, and the roots shallow. The brittle grass crunched under the blade of the shovel. Marking off a two-foot square, I dug it clean and piled the sod and stones in a ridge on the windward side and moved on. Square after square I cleared in this way until I decided strips were more efficient and changed to six-foot paths which I repeated side by side until they were two feet wide. Over and over again I dug my way across — across what? I didn't know. The night sky, normally brilliant with stars, filled with smoke. Only on the farthest horizon over my right shoulder could I see sprinkles of light. I kept my eye on them. They oriented me to the course I must dig across the path of the fire, and they showed me the way to safety in case I had to run.

I had dug and shoveled and piled it seemed an endless number of hours when two little headlights appeared and a truck bumped over the prairie.

"Jump in," the driver yelled. "The wind's turned. We've got to get out of the way."

Throwing my shovel into the truck, I grabbed the sides and pulled myself in.

"For Chrissake, watch where you're puttin' that thing, Pistol. You got my bad foot." Texas Diller! I could have hugged him.

The headlights picking out the worst of the obstacles, the pickup bounded over the prairie, hit a road and sped into the dark.

"What's happening?" I asked. There was no answer

from the obscure, silent figures. "Are we containing it?"
No one replied.

Again the men dropped off one by one, and when it
came my turn, I jumped down with my spade and stood
there waiting for the driver to tell me what to do. He
said nothing. The little truck bounced and banged out
of sight, leaving me once more alone in the night.

I searched the horizon for stars, but the little brilliant
strip above the trees was gone now. I must remember
where the truck had disappeared and set my right
shoulder to it. But what if I dug around in a circle? I
had heard of people, men who were lost and fatigued
beyond endurance, going around in circles and getting
nowhere and finally dying with rescue and safety within
reach. I was tired enough right then, I thought, when
underfoot I felt soft, bare earth. It was the end of a
furrow. Someone had been here and left, maybe at a
wind change which put him in danger, and now that it
was safe again, another had come back. I began to dig
with returning vigor.

The terrain was rougher here. Soon I hit a boulder
too big to move and dug around it, employing it as part
of the sod barrier. The sage proved more difficult. It was
dry and tough, perfect fuel, and I could not shovel it
out. In the distance an ax rang against a tree, and I
thought of asking its wielder to come and hack out the
sage for me, but he had his job, felling trees near the
path of the fire to prevent the flames from rising into
the tops where, enlarged and accelerated, they could
leap from crown to crown far beyond reach. I hacked
and shoveled, clearing what I could, when out of the
dark materialized a team of horses pulling a fresno
guided by a man. I called out. The great steel scoop slid

over the earth and sliced under the boulders and sage, scraping the way clean.

"I could use a grubbing ax."

"I've got one," the driver said, and he gave me the heavy, blunt-nosed tool secured to the harness. He dragged the fresno on, cutting a wide path. "You go forward a ways," he said, " and make a nearer furrow."

Where there was time and men to make them, ribbons of bare earth were best to check the fire and check it again and again, to contain sparks and flaming debris which shot into the air like sky rockets. The team and driver disappeared into the dark.

The smoke, hot and laden with ash, began to bother my breathing. I shoveled more slowly, stopping to rest every few feet. I wondered if anyone knew what anyone else was doing. I sat down on a rock. The ax no longer rang among the trees. The fresno driver's shouts to the team had long ago vanished. I took off my hat and wiped my face and hair and neck with my handkerchief. When I sat still, the silence appalled me. I shoveled another six feet. Maybe the wind had changed and everybody else had gone, but I had been forgotten. My heart banged painfully. I stood very still, trying to sense the nearness of the fire. Should I run? I could see nothing. Then I heard a rattle and bang, and little twin headlights appeared, coming toward me. I watched them. I dropped my shovel and ran for them. The pickup turned. Gunny sacks were pitched out the window without slowing down. I shouted. But the driver didn't hear me. Then caught suddenly against the light, I saw the head, the profile, the nose. I'd know that nose anywhere.

"Conrad!" I yelled. I ran as fast as I could, yelling, "Conrad! Conrad!"

The little truck turned away, rattled, banged, bounced, bounded faster than I could run, and the twin lights disappeared from sight.

I stood still, choking and coughing, maybe crying. I couldn't tell tears from sweat. And the waves of home-sickness and fatigue and loneliness and helpless isola-tion surged over me until my whole body shook from their impact.

"Shovel, damn you," I whispered. "Don't just stand there and bawl."

The smoke and the darkness closed around me. I could no longer tell if I dug my furrow straight on a course against the path of the fire. Leaning, scraping, throwing the shallow sod beyond the bared path, I could make out no landmarks. I sensed nothing familiar in the rocks and sage and meadow grass my shovel hit. Only the wind brought me the message of heat and ash and direction, and it shifted from my cheek to my shoulder to my back and sometimes stopped altogether for min-utes on end, no longer controlling the fire but partly controlled by it.

Turning parallel to my furrow, I saw ahead of me two shades of darkness where the land rose against the sky, and between land and sky a yellow glow boiled up and lit the underbelly of the smoke. If I walked out to a vantage point, perhaps I could tell where I was and where the fire line ran.

The grass crunched underfoot. It was a catastrophe to lose that grass, such as it was, here in the middle of summer, in the middle of a desperate summer in a series of desperate summers. I climbed slowly in the thick air, dragging my spade, and pulled myself wearily to the top of a ridge. There in startled horror I saw the fire.

Fifty, forty, thirty-five yards from me the wave of flame surged toward me, racing up the ridge through the grasses, borne on a wind which swept fiercely upward. I stood immobilized with terror. A lone tree exploded before me and showered me with sparks. My heart banging, the ashen air blocking my lungs, I beat them from my shirt and pants and when I looked up, the whole area was in flames. The grass, the sage, flashed all around me, and the fire line flowed toward me with hypnotizing speed.

For one split second more I was rigid. Then I ran. I ran for the furrow, for beyond the furrow, the wide, deep one the fresno had made. I could feel the fire, the terrible heat, the crackle, the overwhelming smoke, and worse, the panic. Why didn't my legs go faster? I beat, I stamped, I stumbled, I ran, the heat coming through my boots and roasting my back and speeding me onward until I felt the bare earth, the first furrow, then the next, and then the beautiful, wide, deep, smooth, barren swathe the fresno had cut and I dived over it.

I lay there for two seconds, maybe two minutes, gasping and shaking and pressing my face to the ground below the heat and smoke, wondering if I was safe and knowing that it didn't matter much if I wasn't, because I had no other place to go, and I lay there, spread-eagled on the bare earth until I heard a motor approaching.

Another truck appeared. This time a gang rode in it with great oil drums filled to sloshing with water. I hollered and they hollered back, and I ran toward them.

From the first truck Conrad had pitched out bundles of gunny sacks, and now we grabbed them up and plunged them into the drums of water and raced up the hill beyond my furrows. Where the long, wavering line of flames spread, we rushed the fire and beat the flames with the wet gunny sacks. As soon as one was dry, I ran back to the truck and got another. A kind of bucket brigade formed, and the dripping sacks were passed from hand to hand to the beaters along the fire.

Now I could see what I was doing. Day had broken, gray, ash-filled, but day, daylight. I brought the water-heavy burlap down on the flames.

Gradually the fire line disappeared, and the air was filled with steam and smoke. The work slowed. I kicked carefully through the charred grass for sparks.

"Think we got it?" someone asked.

A ranger came down the line, "Great work, boys," he said, repeating it, "great work. We got it this time. You fellows take a break. I'll run you down to Bassetts' to rest up so you'll be fresh later." We scrambled wearily into the back of the truck. I slumped down between two oil drums. My legs suddenly were no longer steady.

The Bassett place lay the closest of all the ranches to the summer range. It was not an ideal ranch because of its remote location, but it had one blessing, an artesian well, the magic of inexhaustible water. My mind could fasten on nothing else.

The water ran out of a six-inch pipe in the front yard, gushing and rolling ice-cold into a shallow wooden trough which stood hip-high, filled it and tumbled through an overflow hole into a stone-lined ditch which carried it off to a stock pond. I was certain I heard the water gushing before I saw the house.

The Bassetts' yard was scattered with people. The ranch women in faded dresses and aprons had gathered there and set up tables and laid out food and drink. A few men stood talking with them, holding a sandwich in one hand and a mug in the other. When the truck stopped and we dropped off, every one of us moved not toward the food but to the trough. No one hurried; no one tried to get there first; we simply moved to the trough and ranged along both sides of it and began to wash. One man plunged his whole head in, and I did, too. The water was like a block of ice. I rubbed my face and my hair and blew like a horse. Another puncher took off his shirt and rubbed his chest and arms with it dripping, wrung it out and put it back on sticking dark and wet to his body. I took off my shirt and did the same, and the sudden icy evaporation against my skin made me shiver violently. Then my whole body began to shake and my fingers trembled as I ran them through my hair, and my knees turned to rubber.

A hand closed tightly on my arm. "Come on," Sam said, "let's get a little food here."

Curls of green lettuce and pink edges of ham stuck out between the layers of white bread in the great stacks of sandwiches. I took two and a crockery mug of coffee which I muddied with tin cow and sweetened with three teaspoons of sugar. Sam and I sat down on a bench against the side of the house and ate and didn't say much.

More trucks left more men in the yard. I saw Conrad drive in with a gang in the back of the pickup with Kincaid Cattle Company stenciled on the door. He saw me and gave me the old high sign, and I waved back, and he drove away.

I had stopped shaking and was thinking of a third sandwich between bracing swallows of coffee when the chief ranger drove up. The chatter and occasional laughter faded away, and everyone turned to him, as he spoke to the men nearest him. Sam and I sat alert and motionless, straining every muscle to hear.

Moving from group to group across the yard, the ranger said, "I think we got it. The wind turned about an hour ago and stayed steady. It's carrying everything right back on itself. We'll need a few boys to stay and mop up, make sure everything's out, but I think we've got it. Thanks a lot, boys, we got it contained, and the wind did the rest." From cluster to cluster of men he went with his soft-spoken, understated words of gratitude. The men looked away or nodded distantly or kidded him in reply. It was everybody's range, and we had worked to save what we could for ourselves. When somebody's in trouble, you help out; it was the old rule of the range, and it had operated once more. When that trouble was one of the furies of nature, then men stood together and fought. Dead beat and slumped on the bench, I turned and grinned at Sam.

"We won," I said.

Sam glanced at me sideways. "We beat the fire, Pistol, but we lost a lot of grass, a lot of grass.

"You take the Model A and gear back," Sam said. "And better tell the places down the road what's happening, and tell Mrs. Gallagher we'll be there about midafternoon. I'll get the boys to trail your horse back."

I took the keys without arguing. I had never been so tired in my life.

The Fall Drive

II

After the fire a shadow fell across the land. I knew it was there, and I refused to let it darken my mind in the magnificence of the best summer of my whole life.

I had taken my place among the men. I was still the youngest and the least experienced, but I was no longer a kid on trial even when I caught hell, which happened every few days.

And there was Allison. Allison Mitchell was my girl. The words rang in my head, a secret that I was never going to tell, when, one night, settling around the open porch, Texas Diller said, "I hear Pistol's got him a woman."

My whole body snapped in surprise.

"That's what comes of lettin' a young buck out nights," Red said. "Keep 'em corralled and they stay out of trouble."

"That's what you old bucks always say," Fonse said. "You just don't want us givin' you no trouble."

It struck me funny that they called Allison a woman. I thought of her as a girl, my girl. Although they recognized three stages for males, kids and boys and men, they conceded only two for females, little girls and women. There wasn't anything in between. Then I began to feel even better. To them I didn't have a girl; I had a woman with all that meant. I looked at Tom, who grinned and blinked and licked his cigarette paper as if he tasted secret pleasures, and I began to wonder, how good can you feel before you bust wide open?

I was so sealed in my own life that I didn't notice what happened around me. Even when Sam gave orders for the fall drive unaccountably early and made no explanation, I paid it no mind, as Texas would say. Sam had us round up almost his entire herd, not only the prime steers and the yearlings but breeding stock as well. Not until then did I take notice. A trace of worry that Sam knew something nobody else knew crossed my mind, that something very serious had happened or was about to happen. Still, it wasn't like Sam to let disaster fall on everybody around him if he could warn them ahead. Still it wasn't like Sam to give unexplained orders. Anxious, I asked Tom about it, and he said, "I just don't know, Pistol." Tom ran his herd with Sam's, and conceivably this gave him the right to ask questions, but you just didn't do it that way. If a man didn't offer an explanation, well, then, you waited. Sam continued unnaturally secretive. The current of uneasiness ran through everyone. Even Texas had fewer ailments in the face of the larger unknown.

There was no time to get to see Allison and tell her that we were about to push off on the big drive. I didn't have two minutes off. One day about noon I found myself alone near the boundary of the Mitchell ranch, and I raced Sundance over there only to have Jeffrey tell me that she was in town with her mother. I wasn't about to leave a message with him, and I was halfway back to Sam's before I thought of writing a note. That day Greasy Granger appeared, and the chuck wagon was hauled out. With spectacular cussing and sweating the old iron cookstove was heaved onto the back and roped into place.

With Tom's steers and culls and the ready stock from Seth's herd the drive grew larger. All night now the bawling echoed over the main ranch. A herd of that size could not be held long in the big pasture. The time to move out was coming; the excitement mounted. On the last morning the chuck boxes were hoisted aboard the wagon, and the bedrolls were heaped high in the wagon bed.

"I'm going to miss you, Billy," Mrs. Gallagher said, when I filled the woodbox for the last time, and she hugged me. Feeling her mattressy bosom against me, I was pleased and embarrassed and hugged her and let go. "This is going to be a mighty lonesome place without you."

Bringing in the remuda on the last morning, I passed Greasy on the wagon road. He had set out ahead to make camp and fire up the cookstove at the place we would reach riding herd that night.

When they were mounted and ready, and the herd was released, Fonse stood up in his stirrups and let out a yell, "O little town, open up those barroom doors, because here I come!"

Sam laughed and rode ahead on his big black. Then the whooping and hollering broke out like Indians.

Ropes came down with resounding smacks on the nearest hides, and slowly, unevenly, reluctantly, the great herd began to move.

I rode all the first day on the western flank of the herd with Tom and Seth. It was only the second drive I had been on. Last year I had to go back to school before the drive, but once for no pay I had ridden with Kincaid's. Now I wanted to pull my weight with the other hands, and I watched Tom and Seth with one eye while I kept the other on the herd. What they did, I did, and I knew it could only be right. Seth had lost the suppleness Tom had, and he was different from Tom in many ways. Tom rode like the human part of his little horse, lithe as a panther, relaxed and so alert that when his horse stumbled and fell, Tom rolled clear in a split second and was back on his feet laughing. Still, they were alike. Their faces had the same set of pleasure; their eyes, squinting against the sun, flickered with satisfaction. They were doing what men of their kind should do, and they knew they did it well. This was the great final act of the season, the drive all the previous work had prepared for, the conclusion before the long dormant winter. It was what prairie men and beasts were meant to do. Watching that pair, I hoped with all my might that I looked just like them, if smaller and younger and not quite so filled out with practice. With them to follow how could I miss?

Before sunup I rounded up the horses. All day I rode with Tom and Seth, pressing the long, scattered procession across the prairie. At night I stood around the fire, listening to the stories before crawling into my bedroll or taking my turn riding night herd under the star-brilliant sky. Eighty miles lay between Sam's place and the stock pens along the Northern Pacific tracks in Great Plain where the cattle were shipped, and eighty miles was a long drive. The first day was like the second, the second like the third, or might have been but for an event which changed everything for the worst.

The third night out Seth did not appear at the chuck wagon. Tom asked me where I saw him last, and I said that he had gone off to the west after some strays around maybe three o'clock. Everyone stirred uneasily.

"He'll show up," Sam said, but in the morning when I rode out to wrangle the horses, I found Seth's horse grazing among them. Saddled, bridled, the reins dragging, the horse nibbled calmly from clump to clump.

I wheeled and raced for the camp, only pulling up after the first wild dash when I realized that they would need the horses to find him. I raced back again, around the herd and, moving in on them, I caught Seth's horse by the reins. The others I pushed ahead of me as fast as they would go.

As I approached the camp, I was clearly visible driving the herd down the piece of wagon road. The whole crew gathered around me.

"Where'd you find him, Pistol?" Tom said.

"He was right with the remuda."

"Where was that?" Sam asked. I told him.

Tom inspected the horse for sign. Certain thistles caught in the saddle blanket, certain burrs low in the tail or high in the mane, said something of where he had been. In the end he said, "No sign."

"He must have dragged the reins," Sam said, his lips tight. "Tom, you take Pistol here. You can find him. You should be back by night."

While I ate what Greasy Granger heaped on my tin

plate, Tom rolled his soogans, tucking inside a canteen and a coffee can which he packed with tea bags, Oxo cubes and sugar lumps. By the time he tied the saddle strings around the roll, I was ready. In silence we set out southwest.

Tom rode a little ahead of me, watching the earth directly ahead of us and scanning the distance. "Take that ridge, Pistol," he said to me, and I rode to the crest of a rise and searched a hidden coulee and returned. "Anything?" he said. "Nothing," I said.

The cattle had not been driven over this section. The earth was dry. No rain had fallen. A bridled horse with the reins dragging will hold his head to the side, and the sliding tracks were reasonably easy to follow. How much ground he had covered was more difficult. He wandered. He stopped to browse. He spent the night in a sheltered draw. When we found this spot, Tom groaned, "Oh, that's bad."

My stomach gave way. Coyotes, vultures, rodents could beset an injured man in the night. We hastened faster across the pine-scattered hills.

Coming over a ridge almost together, we saw him.

"Oh, Jesus, there he is!" Tom cried out.

Below us among the rocks lay Seth McCollum. The horses scrambled down the slope, and Tom was dismounting before his little horse came to a stop. He rushed to the crumpled figure.

"My God, Seth, what's happened?" he whispered. "Pistol, he's alive. Bring the bedroll. Half his ribs is kicked in. He got throwed or kicked or something. Seth, can you talk?"

The blood-traced eyes were half open. From the corner of his mouth a cascade of phlegm and blood reached the ground. Tom wiped it away, gently, with his bandanna handkerchief. I unrolled the soogans beside the old man.

"Ease him in," Tom said, and together we lifted him. "Keep him level. God knows what's broke inside him." He wasn't heavy for all his length, and I noticed his hands again with the long fingers like twigs wrapped in parchment flesh, the backs covered with dark spots from the weathering of decades. Carefully we folded the quilts and canvas over him.

"Pistol, you stay with him." Tom gripped my shoulder. "I'm going back for the wagon. Stir up a fire and make some tea with plenty of sugar in it and then make some broth. Make as much as he'll drink, and I'll be back." He swung into the saddle, turned his horse up the gully, and disappeared over the ridge at a high trot.

The pine twigs were so dry and flammable that the trick was to make a fire hot enough to boil the water I poured from the canteen into the coffee can. I surrounded the little blaze with stones to reflect the heat inward on itself and pushed the fire into a smaller and smaller area until at last little air bubbles rose from the bottom. I called that boiling and dropped in the tea bag. As I waited, I glanced toward the old man. Had he moved? Was he watching me? All his movements at work had been sternly economical. Surely he wouldn't waste any now. I put three sugar lumps in the cup of tea and knelt beside him.

"This is hot, Seth," I said, wondering if he should have it hot. "It's tea. I made some tea, Seth."

I wiped the bloody phlegm from the corner of his mouth.

He signed it away.

"But, Seth, you need it. You've been here two days without anything. You've got to take it."

The eyes closed in refusal.

"You need the liquid." I opened his lips and parted the yellowed teeth and spooned the tea down his throat. He growled, returning tea and blood and phlegm to his lips, which I wiped again. I lifted his head and poured swallows between the dried lips, but he refused to open his teeth and the liquid dribbled out. I stirred up some broth double strength over the fire, and lifting his head again, I begged him to take it. The old eyes regarded me without the least interest. The teeth refused to open. "I can't help you, Seth," I yelled at him. "I can't help you if you won't let me." Then I eased his head down to the quilts as I began to shake all over. Oh, Christ, Tom, hurry up.

Never had the surrounding rubble hills struck me so oppressively. The loneliness, the silence, the hostility to every form of life, nothing flew or crawled or scampered through the emptiness on every side.

The clip of horse's hooves filled the vacancy of sky and coulee. I ran toward the sound, shouting, "Tom, he won't take anything, he won't drink, Tom, I think . . ." Tom looked into my face hard and anxiously. Then he ran to the old man and knelt beside him. He lifted the cup of broth and then set it down and turned away. Our eyes met, and he whispered, "Pistol, he's dyin'."

Protest came up in me, pressing against my teeth until suddenly my jaw locked against the tears and fright and anguish I could not at that moment bear. Tom made a move as if to grip my arm, and I froze. If he touched me, I'd break out crying, but he only reset his hat, saying, "We'll do what we can, Pistol. The wagon's comin'."

I found Seth's hat among the rocks and with the firewood we no longer needed propped it up to shade his face. The sun was high now, and as always hot. I don't know when Seth died. He didn't give a death rattle or a final twitching. After a while Tom seemed to notice a difference, and he found him dead. Not long afterwards Greasy drove up with the wagon, and the three of us laid Seth in the cocoon of soogans in the wagon bed. His old-timer's hat I placed on his chest. Then we mounted and trailed the wagon back to the herd.

The drive was already on the move. One by one the men drifted in, when they saw the wagon, made inquiry, and went back to the herd. Nobody said much until Sam said he would take the body into town. Texas said we should bury him right there where he lived, and Red said, "You'd like to see him laid out like a Sioux, just to dry up and bleach, but we ain't got no squaw to set with him and keep the coyotes off." No one argued after that, and Sam and Greasy set off for the road to hail down the first passing truck. The punchers closed the gap — Fonse moved over to our side — and the drive continued. It was not the same. The shadow had reached us.

When we entered the long plain which declined to the confluence of the two rivers, when I saw the town marked out in the distance under its canopy of dust, I was relieved. The town was there. Some permanent thing inhabited the great emptiness. The shining rails pierced the town from each side. The sun gleamed on the power lines looping across the land. It was a relief to see them.

Bellering and bawling, the cattle milled in the ford of the river. We pressed the long procession into the water to drink their long, thirsty fill before they crossed to the stockyards and the weighing scales. They would stay there quite a while without much tending. I rode to Tom and Fonse. "Do you want to swim in the flumes?"

They eyed me sideways.

"Those chutes that carry the irrigation ditch over the river?" Fonse said.

"How do you swim in those?" Tom asked.

"All the kids in town swim in them," I said. "You let the water carry you through and then you work your way back, and do it again."

"Well, I'm hot enough and dirty enough," Tom said, "to give it a try. Come on, Fonse, you can be lifeguard."

"Me?" Fonse croaked. Tom took his saddle strings and hit the rump of Fonse's horse, and the three of us raced headlong across the prairie to the point where the aqueduct began. Texas Diller raced up behind us just as we hauled to a stop, and he stared at me as I swung off, left the reins to drag, and ripped off my dirty shirt. He said, "Jesus, Tom, are you goin' into that thing?"

Tom said, "Sure, why not?" hopping on one foot and pulling a boot off.

"Why not?" murmured Fonse. "I can think of a reason."

"Why, I'd just let myself stink to the last day before I'd climb up there," Texas said. "You can pull my teeth, shoot my foot off, fill me with moonshine, but you ain't never ever goin' to get me in that."

I was about to climb up the scaffold when I looked at Tom and started to laugh. He stood in the dust stark naked and ready to argue with Texas, and his body was as white as bleached bone. The years of Levi's and long johns had rubbed the hair from his legs, and the sandy-brown patches on his body stood out against his white skin. He was all white but for his hands to the wrist and his face to his eyebrows and his neck to a leather-brown V at its base. No man alive looks funnier than a cowboy without his gear on.

"Cut the laughin', Pistol," he yelled at me, "or you're a goner."

I raced up the scaffold with Tom after me, jumped into the water, and was swept with incredible speed through the flume.

"Oh, Christ," Tom hollered and jumped in behind me. "My God, I'm goin' to drown," he yelled. "Who pulled the plug on this bathtub?"

The water swept over me and around me. It carried me like a chip to the other side of the river where I caught hold of a crossbeam above my head, stopped my course, and hauled myself hand over hand, from crossbeam to crossbeam, back to the start. Fonse was there looking over the edge and down into the water.

"I just don't feel like drownin' today," he said. Tom and I laughed, let go of the strut and sailed down the flume again.

We shot the flumes again and again, sailing with the current and fighting our way back against it like salmon in their chutes, until the pads of my fingers wrinkled.

We hung from a strut and rested.

"That's the first time I've ever seen a man die," I said. "I'd thought it was different, I mean, Seth wouldn't take anything. He didn't fight. He wouldn't let me help him, Tom."

"He didn't want any help, Pistol. I've seen a couple of animals die like that. They wouldn't eat, wouldn't drink more than a little. They just figured it was time to die, I guess, and didn't make no fuss about it." Tom grinned at me, and after a while I said, "I don't know if that makes dying not so scary or scarier than ever."

"I don't know, either," Tom said.

"Do you think we should have buried him where we found him? It was where he had lived."

"I've heard that song both ways," Tom said. " 'Bury me not' and 'Bury me out on the lone prair-ee, where the coyotes howl and the wind blows free.' "

"Which would you choose for yourself, I mean?"

"The lone prair-ee, I reckon," and he grinned at me.

When we drove the herd into the pens, our whoops and hollers went unanswered. The stockyards were oddly quiet. They seemed to be operating with a skeleton crew. Sam was there, and he strode toward Tom. His face was set. He rested his hand on the neck of Tom's horse and looked up into Tom's face.

He said, "The bank folded. Yesterday."

The End of My World

12

I dragged my saddle up the porch steps and dropped it beside the front door. All kinds of fatigue drained me dry. I pushed the bell a couple of times and opened the door and called out, "Anybody home?" In the second of silence that followed I felt it. The house was weighted with anxiety.

Conrad came into the hall from the kitchen, halfway laughing. "Disaster has struck, buddy boy."

"I heard about it."

"Oh, I'll bet."

"Sam told us when we got into the yards. Where's Mom?"

"Oh, Billy, is that you? Is that you?" She rushed from the kitchen and into my arms. "I was hoping you'd come home, oh, Billy, Billy."

"Oh, come on, Mom." Laughing, I wiped her eyes with her apron, "You didn't miss me that much." Over her head, I said, "Have you been down to the bank?

What'd Mr. Dostal say, how'd he explain closing it down?"

My mother sank into a kitchen chair and pressed her hand to her mouth.

"Mr. Dostal didn't do any explaining," Conrad said. "They found him floating in the Yellowstone this morning." Conrad laughed his short, bitter laugh.

"Oh, Jesus," I laughed, that unsuppressible haw-haw at death. It wouldn't stop until I inhaled a long breath and sat down with a thump.

"It's better than being lynched."

"Oh, Conrad," my mother cried out, "you always think of the horrible things, the horrible things."

"Where's Dad?"

"Billy, go downtown and find him."

"He's at the dogger plant, Mom," Conrad said, but she ignored him. "Find him, Billy. You can't tell what a man will think of."

Conrad laughed shortly. "The old man isn't going to jump in the Yellowstone. He hasn't got the nerve."

"Conrad!" she screamed.

I patted her shoulder. "Take it easy, Mom. He's all right. I'll go down and see. Come on, big shot. You're no help around here."

All my savings were in that bank, what I had left from being a paper boy and what I saved out at Sam's last year. They couldn't actually be gone.

The stores were open, although no business was being done. People thronged the street, wandering up and down, gathering in knots, squatting against the storefronts to roll a cigarette and exchange comment, standing at the door of the bank, waiting.

What about Sam, I wondered. Would there be any money coming? But of course there would be. The cattle were consigned to St. Paul and Chicago, and if Sam had not been paid at the Great Plain pens, he would eventually receive his share from the commission men in the Eastern yards. Sometime or other, if not now, Sam would pay off. I wasn't really worried, after I thought about it.

But my savings, it looked as if they were gone for good. A small crowd of men stood in front of the bank, some with their backs to the door, more interested now in what was said than in the possibility of the doors being unlocked. As we came to the edge of the crowd, Mr. Delaney, the car dealer, said, "It isn't going to open, boys, but there's no cause for alarm. This bank is as safe as any bank in Montana, you know that." He stepped backwards onto the steps between the tall, fluted pilasters. "We don't know why it's locked. The examiners are coming, and we'll find out, and the chances are we'll get our money out."

The crowd silently regarded the speaker, considering his words, until someone spoke up, "That doesn't tell us why Bob took to the river. If everything is okay, he'd be here to say so."

"I've known Bob all my life," Mr. Delaney said. "We were the both of us born right here. We grew up together. I know him, I knew him as well as I know my brother, and I've never caught him with his hand in the till. I'd like to meet the man who has."

After this came silence again, a believing and disbelieving silence.

"When are the examiners coming, Pete?"

"They're on their way. I don't know the exact time of

day, boys, but they're coming. I know they've left the Twin Cities."

"The Twin Cities!"

A new tone shot through the crowd.

"What do you mean, the Twin Cities? Bob Dostal owns this bank."

Mr. Delaney said, "He sold out awhile back, but . . ."

The crowd tensed with anger. "If I'd've known that, I would've took my money out of here long before this."

"Now wait a minute, boys, Bob . . ."

"The dirty son of a bitch, he tricked us."

"Hold on there . . ."

"We'd never go along with those Eastern fellows, and he knew it."

"Of course, he knew it, boys, but maybe he had to sell out, maybe he had to, to save anything. We don't know the whole story."

Mr. Delaney stepped down into the crowd again. "There's no use arguing. I'll stand you fellows a round of coffee in the Chinaman's cafe." They followed Mr. Delaney across the street and disappeared into the Chinaman's place, leaving Conrad and me to stare after them.

"Come on," I said. "We'd better find him."

"Oh, hell, he's all right."

Still, Conrad moved with me.

"Seth McCollum died on the drive," I said.

Conrad speeded up, staring at me. "You're kidding."

I shook my head. "I was with him."

Conrad groaned. "Oh, God. Everything's dying around here."

A tremor that death could be catching hit me, and I loped ahead. "Come on."

The high sun, the dust in the streets now stirred by the drying wind into the small cones of dust devils dancing over the pavement, the parched figures in dusty boots, the still and empty stores standing with doors open, such were the elements of the town the day the bank folded. It was not a landscape of life but of some replica in hell.

On the corner where the street came up from the tracks and the stock pens we met my father returning from the dogger plant. I studied his face, and I figured he was anxious but not that anxious.

"We're going to hold out," he said, his teeth tight. "Pete Delaney knows where he can get some money, and we're going to hold out."

Relief rushed through me, over me like water in the flumes, and I grinned at him. "Oh, that's great," I said, "I knew there was a way."

My father clapped me on the shoulder. "There's always a way," he said grimly. "There has to be." Turning, we walked together down the main street. Conrad said nothing.

What the summer left behind, the fall winds incinerated. The everlasting grasses, the grama, the blue stem, the tufts of buffalo and foxtail, were scorched to the ground. What cattle could survive this time, I wondered and I thought I understood why Sam had sold off almost his whole herd.

Day became night, and night, day. Men and women holding the hands of stilled children walked the sidewalks. Everyone waited, listening, watching with a sense of foreboding, but nothing happened. Night turned to day, the temperature dipped, school opened, there was Allison.

Dressing for school, Conrad said, "For cry yi, what's taking you so long? You only have to be clean."

"That may be enough for you," I said, "but it's not for me."

"Fancy Dan," he growled in disgust. I continued to survey my shirts and decided on the red-striped one.

Richie Greatbear, Sonny Goldstein, Hack Davis, Raf Gomez, all the kids I knew and had known all my life, churned up and down the high school corridors, laughing, hollering, pounding each other, eyeing new developments in the girls who swept past in rows, commenting, oh, boy, and, I don't think she's ever going to get any, making the tough teachers more cruel and fearsome if you got one and playing them down if you had one last year. I stationed myself by a corner window near Allison's locker, leaning on the radiator, and waited, talking and laughing and watching the stairs and the halls both ways and waiting for my lovely girl, so cool and warm, open and secret, her brown eyes serious and gay, and thinking, what if your best friend is a girl, wondering if such a thing was possible. The bell rang.

I watched for her all day, but she didn't come. I waited at the window the following day, but her locker stayed vacant. It stayed vacant the next and the next. On Friday I knew it was true. Allison wasn't coming. The blue envelope waited for me on the hall table, when I got home, and I ripped it open: "Oh, Billy, why didn't you come? I waited and waited. Then I missed you the day you came, and I waited and waited some more. I rode over to Sam's one day, but you had already gone. When I got to town, I called you, but you weren't home yet. Mother and Daddy have sent me to school here near Chicago. I wanted to go, early in the summer, but then I changed my mind, but they said it was too late. I guess I like it, but it is so different, and, Billy, I haven't met anyone like you." I folded the letter twice so that it fit into my shirt pocket without showing.

The whole world took on the aspect of a game where nobody knew the rules. When I tried the old moves that had worked, they worked no longer. About once a week I stopped in at the Laurel and turned on my broadest grin and asked, "Need a sweeper today?" The manager continued to rock in the hickory rocker brought in from the veranda. "Not today." I knew he swept the place himself. I tried Acton's, but Acton's no longer delivered. "Anybody who's sick enough for a prescription just goes ahead and dies," old man Acton told me. "Of course, I'm selling some Perry Davis' Painless Pain Killer and Dr. Pfunder's Pills, but that's to customers on the hoof." I could not bring myself to go into the saddlery, not after the first time, because it was the saddest place of all. The craftsmen who were left bent over their meager work with dogged faces which said to me, what else do I know, where else can I go? Even the odors of leather and hemp had faded. My best luck came at the feedlots where the commission man yelled at me sometimes, "Grab a pitchfork, Billy, that son of a bitch didn't show up today." And exulting, I grabbed a pitchfork and fed and watered the captive critters and made a couple of bucks before some rummy cowpoke, bleary eyes and swollen jaw, appeared.

The first week in November I made a ringing speech

in the assembly, calling on all good students to come to the aid of their country, change horses in the middle of the stream, and elect the great governor of the state of New York. Anybody who could run a state which was darkened by skyscrapers and swarmed with people plodding to the soup kitchens, I said, in making my most believable point, could run the United States of America. The applause thundered, and afterwards, Mr. Burbank said, "Just a point of information, but there is a small part of Manhattan Island where there are skyscrapers. New York State is largely dairyland and old manufacturing cities." I eyed him doubtfully, and he said, "You must go there sometime."

Roosevelt's election sent hope surging through the whole community. Something would be done now. My father was noticeably more cheerful around the house until the news about the bank broke. The doors were to reopen, nobody knew when, but inside no money waited for anyone or any business. Mr. Dostal, it seemed, had juggled the books.

"He was a crook," Conrad said.

"No, he wasn't a crook," my father told him, patiently. "He knew things were bad long ago, he knew it first, way before the rest of us."

"Everybody downtown says he was crooked as a stick."

"They don't know everything where you hang out," said my father with bitterness. "Bob Dostal tried to keep us all going as long as he could. He thought things would pick up; he'd been through some bad times before, and they always took a turn for the better after a while. He and Pete Delaney did everything they could to keep this town going."

"Dad," I said, "did he get his money out?"

"Bob Dostal didn't get a thing."

"I mean Mr. Delaney. Everybody says he pulled his out when he saw what was coming, and that's why . . ."

"All that's vicious gossip," he spoke angrily. "Pete Delaney has always banked out of the Twin Cities. He never had everything in the bank here."

"But why did he do that? He always says you should boost your home town, and everybody hates the Twin Cities."

"I don't know, son," he said, vastly tired. "Maybe he did it just in case . . ." and his voice trailed away.

"He wasn't so dumb," Conrad said and flicked on the Atwater Kent radio. Under cover of the din and static and my father yelling, "Not so loud!" he muttered, "A damn sight smarter than anybody else," but only I heard him.

The long freight trains wound into the Great Plain yards, crying out their long, lonely woe-woe in the frigid nights. Once the freight yard crew found a drifter frozen stiff in one of the empties. I didn't see him. Raf Gomez's father worked on a section gang. Raf told me. I wondered what made anybody ride the rods through Montana in the dead of winter, but maybe they didn't know where they were going, had just hopped a freight in the Chicago yards and gone with it.

In the early part of the new year a heavy snow pack raised some talk of better grass next season, but mostly the news concerned frozen cattle and hospital herds and how the stores of hay bales and cottonseed cake filled the warehouses, but nobody could buy them in sufficient quantities, nobody but Terence Mitchell who sent Jeffrey in, driving a new truck, a number of times during the winter.

One night after school, slogging through the mush left by the chinook, I saw the truck parked in the drive of the Mitchell house. It was my chance to hear more about Allison. I made a turn toward the house, trying to look aimless in case any buddies were watching, went around to the back door where Jeffrey would most likely be, and bumped into Mr. Mitchell coming out the door.

"Hello, Billy," he said, gripping my hand. His walrus moustache seemed unusually stiff in the cold, and his sheepskin coat made him look extra burly.

"Hi, Mr. Mitchell," I smiled weakly. "I thought maybe Jeffrey was here, and I wondered how — everything is up around Punkin Creek." I found I didn't like him much anymore.

"I was just leaving, but come in. Come in." He led the way through the back hall, the large kitchen as big as our living room, through the butler's pantry with the metal sink and the silver gleaming behind the glass doors and into the dark dining room. "I suppose you're too young for a sherry," he said, pouring a glass from a bottle on the sideboard, and waved me into the living room. He pulled open the draperies on two windows and we sat down in the chill and dusty room.

"How's the winter been out there?" I asked. I disliked the sureness of his manner. Nothing could touch him.

"Not too bad, Billy. The snow has been steady and the cold hasn't let up till this chinook. We had a hospital herd of close to one hundred in January, but we made it through with very few losses, considering. The cottonseed cake and hay did it, of course."

"How about Allie Bassett and Dominic Arlo?" I asked. The rumor circulated that Mr. Mitchell had loaned them what they needed, loaned cottonseed cake to be paid back at some unspecified time, but I didn't dare ask the question outright so I watched his face for a sign of the rumor's truth.

"I think they're making it," he said. He sipped his sherry and dabbed at his moustache. I could tell nothing.

"Is Sam okay?"

His face grew more serious, and he shook his head. "I haven't seen Sam all winter," and I thought, good, Sam wouldn't take his crumbs, he'd starve first. "I don't know, but I suppose he is. Well! It's nice to see you, Billy." He stood up and clapping me on the shoulder, he moved me through the dining room toward the back door. "Allison asked about you in her last letter."

I wondered if he could feel my shoulder tighten under his hand and I said, "Is she having a good time back — there?" and he said, "I think so, but she misses the ranch and the wide-open spaces."

Mr. Mitchell and I parted in the driveway, and a few minutes later down the street he passed me in the new truck. Watching it go by, it was dark blue and the radiator was curved backwards, streamlining, the ads called it, and it was brand-new, I wondered how Mr. Mitchell could buy it, when no one else could. Maybe his remittance from England, maybe that was it; in which case the moral was: have outside resources. Mr. Delaney had his bank in St. Paul, and he was still solvent. The rest were wiped out. All the home-town boosters and the penny-ante storekeepers and shoestring ranchers had been reduced to beggars, petitioners for crumbs from the smart guys' tables. Even Allie Bassett and Dominic Arlo, who had appeared to me self-sufficient, independent men who could take care of themselves no matter what, were compelled to accept favors. My father was taking Mr. Delaney's money to keep the dogger plant open, but that was different. With Mr. Dostal they were investors, and my father's investment was to run the place. Now that Mr. Dostal was dead, Mr. Delaney put up the cash, and my father kept working. It was an investment; it wasn't charity.

I reached home, and my mother said, "Billy, will you go down to LeJoi's and pick up the groceries for me?"

I said, "Okay. Give me some money."

She turned away from me and said, "Mr. LeJoi is letting us charge everything for a while."

I could hardly breathe. The silence was dense between us. I couldn't bring myself to ask the real question, and I said, "The Safeway's cheaper."

"Just go to Mr. LeJoi's," she said.

The Safeway was also cash.

I saw myself going into LeJoi's dark little store and walking out with a big brown paper bag under the eyes of Mrs. LeJoi and maybe one of the guys who would notice I didn't pay.

"I've got a lot of homework," I said. "Maybe Conrad will go when he gets here."

"He's upstairs."

It was very clear. Conrad would not go. The silence grew thick and heavy; it acquired a crushing weight like water. I didn't move.

"The list is on the table," she said.

In some way compelled, I picked up the scrap of paper and went out. It was three blocks to LeJoi's. I crossed the backyard to the alley, on fire with rage and hate for my mother who made me do this because she couldn't bring herself to it, and when I realized this, the rage passed over her, leaving only pity behind, and I loathed Conrad with all my heart and soul. He couldn't face it, either, Conrad, the tough guy, but I could not pity him, because he made me the sucker. I made myself the sucker. Why did I pick up the list? Nobody forced me. I just didn't have any guts. Conrad had told me a thousand times that I was a mealymouth, always trying to please, always saying, gee, that's great, and now I got what I deserved, the dirtiest job of all.

I walked past the store. A ridge of dirty snow still edged the sidewalk, the accumulation of Mr. LeJoi's winter shoveling. Oh, God, I had to do it, and I spun around and rushed the door.

From behind the counter Mrs. LeJoi looked up and eyed me sourly as she wrote items on a pad. Sonny Goldstein waited in front of her.

We exchanged a strangled greeting, and I dived into the dim interior of the store. I didn't want Sonny to know. His father was probably doing all right, not the jewelry and the agates maybe but the pawnshop part. It was the right business to be in. Consulting the list, I pulled items from the shelves, packets of navy beans and split peas and macaroni, peeking down the dark aisle to see if Sonny had gone. I didn't want him hanging around, waiting for me while I checked out. Finally, the door slammed and I looked quickly to see that he had gone, which he had, and I carried my box of groceries to the counter.

Mrs. LeJoi looked at me in anger and said nothing, only turned back the leaf of the pad marked, "S. Goldstein," folded it under, wrote "Catlett" on the clean gray soft paper and began to list the items. The Goldsteins must be in the same fix, I thought, and felt relief

155

and a wave of disgust at my relief. I should be glad if somebody else had better luck. The pad, I noticed, had a great many pages turned under.

I summoned my speech and squawked, "I want to charge it." She looked up from her pad and her scorn burned my face.

"You and everybody else," she said. "My old man has gone soft in the head. If Roosevelt can't do anything, how can Lee-Joy, answer me that."

I wished I'd kept my mouth shut.

"Well, Roosevelt just took office March fourth," I said. "I guess he's got to have a little time."

"He'd better hurry up," she growled, "Or it's Dead Horse Gulch for this state."

I nodded and muttered thanks or something and went out. It was the first of many exchanges with that caustic and overpowering woman, for I became the boy who always ran that miserable, degrading errand.

Spring brought an upswing of optimism no one had felt since the election. The snow pack had taken its toll, but as it receded, it left the prairie moist and spongy. The tough, drought-resistant grasses sprang up with refreshed vitality, and the others, the ones no one had seen for years now, the parched and stunted growths, the little patches that looked like nothing but dead roots, burst into life and grew. Rain fell. Maybe the drought was over. Men were cautious, but one thing we knew, the winter was gone, and the cold, damp winds of spring blew over a new and unbelievable green.

I felt certain that the drought was a thing of the past. Wasn't the prairie greener, more lush than at any time since I had worked at Sam's place? These things went in cycles and always had. There was the story of Joseph in the Bible to prove it, and the new Secretary of Agriculture in Washington was saying the same thing. The business of the prairie would settle back to normal, into its own cycle of riding circle, roundup and branding, grazing and the big fall drive, into its familiar turn of days in the saddle and nights at the main ranch or in camps on the summer range.

I planned to go back out to Sam's, and I kept looking for him or for his Model A, and I made my way home from school each day as the spring advanced past the places where I knew he went. The feedstore, the pens by the NP tracks, the express office, the Safeway, the saddlery, the Plainsman. Maybe I should have guessed what was coming the afternoon I passed the Plainsman and Tom hurtled through the door and crashed into me. Embraced, we staggered toward the curb and then back to thump into the bar door. At first I thought he knew me and hugged me in boozy affection, and I began to laugh, "Tom, it's me, Pistol."

"Don' shoot," he said.

We staggered toward the curb again while I tried to hold all two hundred pounds of him upright. "Tom, hey, listen, it's me. Billy Catlett." He reared back and glared at me. For a second I was scared he would swing. He stepped forward, passed out cold and fell on me. We slumped to the sidewalk together.

Several passersby stopped and laughed, watching me squirm and heave and push my way out from under two hundred pounds deadweight. I stood up and glared blackly at them, and they moved on, leaving me alone and wondering what to do.

Old Horace, the bartender, put his head out and said, "Just leave him be. He's been like this for two months now. It's not the first time I've called the pokey to come get him."

I said nothing. Leave him be, out cold on the sidewalk, alone and abandoned? I couldn't do it, and I squatted against the building, never looking up at anyone who went by, until the cops came and bore him away.

The next day I borrowed the car and set out for Sam's.

As I crossed it, I looked out through the windshield at the greening prairie. I had never seen such a beautiful color. The severe winter had helped, and then the rain. The buffalo grass had come back, and the blue stem, which had once covered this land like wheat, reappeared in the wetter places. The gumbo soil shone a shade darker on the road, around the prairie dog holes, between the spreading shrubs of sage. Just to see the prairie greening up lightened my spirits. Everything would be all right again.

Turning off the main road, crossing the cattle guard under Sam's gate, I followed the little winding lane to the top of the hill where I could look down on the main ranch. It was beautiful and still, like a calendar picture, strangely still, almost deserted. I gunned the engine and raced down the hill.

The yard was empty. There was no Model A coupe around. No sound came from the corrals. I banged on the kitchen door. Silence inside. I banged louder and longer. Did I hear someone stirring? I banged again and again and again. After a while the door opened. It was Roscoe.

"Howdy," he said, and I said, "Howdy."

After a minute I said, "Is Sam around?"

Roscoe came out of the house and squatted on the ground, rolling a cigarette. "Sam's gone," he said.

I stared at him. "Gone where?"

"Gone to California, I guess."

I squatted in stunned silence. "Did — did he sell the place? Did he sell the rest of the stock? The horses? Did he sell Sundance?"

"Some stock's left, but he sent the horses to auction."

"Sundance is gone?"

"That's right, Pistol."

I swallowed. "Is Sam coming back?"

"I dunno. He asked me to take care of the place and try and get it through the summer, and that's what I'm doin'. Did you want him for something?"

I stared into the circling hills in shocked silence. Sam was gone; Sundance was gone; everything was gone. I had come out for room and board and twenty dollars a month because room and board and twenty dollars a month was salvation. There was nothing for me here.

Out of the silence Roscoe said, "Maybe Tom needs a rider over to his place."

Startled, I looked at him. The flickering piglet eyes showed no change of expression, no particular interest. It crossed my mind that Tom probably didn't have a place anymore; he had to pay for those drinks with something. Whether Roscoe knew this, I couldn't tell, and I nodded, murmuring, "Maybe at Tom's."

"There's the Mitchell place," he said, and I nodded again, knowing I wouldn't go there. I would never take the crumbs from that lord's table.

When I turned the car and drove away, back over the road I had come, I saw the sweet new green, the returning buffalo grass, the native blue joint sprouting

along the creek beds, the sage fragrant in the unaccustomed moisture, and I knew that the whole greening
prairie came too late.

As soon as I knew this, I found it unbearable and I
pulled a shade in my mind to keep my new and certain
knowledge hidden from my inner view.

I slept late the next morning, a dead deep sleep, and
when I came downstairs I found my father sitting alone
in the living room.

"You're kind of late for work," I said.

At first he didn't answer, and then he said, "Billy, I
want to talk with you."

All my blood drained into my shoes. I forgot my
morning appetite and I sank into a chair. We faced each
other across the dim room, and we waited a long time in
silence.

Finally I asked, "Did it close down?"

Did I see him nodding his head? Yes, he was nodding,
shifting in the overstuffed plush chair, and then he said,
"Yes, Billy, it shut down last night."

I nodded, too, I don't know why. In the dim room we
sat there, both nodding, and my father said it again,
"We closed the doors last night."

I waited, my mind behind the curtain.

"The money ran out," he said. "That's about all
there is to it. With what we could keep selling and what
Pete Delaney kept putting into it, we got through the
winter until . . ."

We lapsed into silence again.

Then he said, "Billy, I hope you can understand all
this."

I nodded, but somehow speech wouldn't come.

"Billy," he said, and I waited. "Billy, the money ran

out some time back. Pete's money, but I wanted to keep it going till spring, into the summer. I thought . . . well, I thought things would pick up."

I could hear him breathing now through his mouth.

"So," he said, "I went into debt."

My lips parted for air.

"They're going to take the car, the furniture, everything I've got."

When he could speak again, he said, "Billy, I hope you can understand all this. I hope you can forgive me."

"Gee, what's there to forgive?" I said. "Sure I can." But I understood nothing, I heard nothing but the words and they were shells empty of meaning.

He stood up and put his hand on my shoulder. "You'd better get some breakfast," he said. "I'm glad I can talk to you, Billy, glad I can talk to you." He patted my shoulder, and suddenly I felt like crying.

PART TWO

Sundown

The Pieces

13

They took everything. They stripped us bare. When they came to possess, they took everything that wasn't nailed down. They took the car from where it sat closed into the little houselike garage out in back. They took the overstuffed chair, the overstuffed sofa, the bent-necked bridge lamp, and the Atwater Kent in its scratched mahogany cabinet. They rolled up the worn Wilton rug and carried it out. They took the bureaus from the upstairs bedrooms and the rusty ice skates from the basement. They took anything that could bring in fifty cents, and they would have taken our clothes, too, if we hadn't hidden them behind the shelves of empty Mason jars in the fruit cellar.

Or, rather, they would have taken everything, if my father hadn't stopped them. When they put their hands on the round kitchen table, he rested his hand on it and said, "Leave us something, boys." Just those words, simply said, no emotion, no sniveling, only, "Leave us something, boys."

They set down the table and not looking at my father, the one in the wide suspenders said, "They'll never know."

They left us the old round table and the oak chairs and the stove and the beds. They couldn't take the house, which my father had always rented.

We stood there, shock still. We had stopped thinking. We were too numb to think. We were afraid there was nothing to think of so we thought of nothing.

"I am glad," my mother's voice trembled, and she tilted her chin. "I am glad they left us the beds."

Conrad snorted, "Oh, Mom," and then tenderly, "oh, Mom."

She held up an old red sock, one I had worn in third grade. Her hand shook so that it jingled. "I had it under the mattress all the time."

I had to laugh. She was like a little kid.

Tears now tumbled from her eyes, and she almost babbled, "I learned that from my father. That's the way they came through the great Chicago fire. His mother always kept a sock under the mattress. She gave it to him when the fire came close and told him to run down to the lake and bury it in the sand. And he did." She was sobbing horribly now and holding up the sock and shaking it. "And when everything else was burned up and they had lost everything, he went back and found it."

My father turned his back and stared out the window.

My mother threw back her head and drew in great, hoarse, terrifying sobs.

Well, we got used to it. The footsteps echoing, voices

ricocheting. I thought I knew that old four-square frame house, but now I knew it as I had never known it before. Nothing about it was hidden. There was nothing to hide.

The only room with life in it was the kitchen, and there were smells, steam, bubbling pots, stale coffee, once-used tea leaves carefully spread out on a towel to dry, yesterday's corn bread securely wrapped. Among these my mother worked. She nourished her kitchen the way a cowhand caught out on the prairie nurses a fire against the elements.

My father sat on the front porch, all morning, all afternoon, all evening. It was dim and shaded, the coolest place, and he sat there without moving much, just shifting his position in the oak chair he brought out from the kitchen. He nodded to me when I went by and occasionally spoke.

At night we gathered around the old kitchen table, and we boys stood behind our chairs until my mother had put everything on the table and made one or two jumps to get something she forgot, until my father said, "Conrad, seat your lady mother," which he did, and we could sit down. Whatever it was, chili and beans, macaroni and cheese, a stew of stringy meat and carrots, we ate in silence. Conrad said nothing. A smile always played around his mouth, a sickening one-sided cynical smirk.

When he finished, he got up and wiped his mouth, which still twisted to one side, and went out and slammed the back screen behind him.

The slam died, and his footsteps on the stoop faded away across the dry backyard. My mother burst into tears.

"This is just a boardinghouse to him," she sobbed. "It isn't his home anymore at all."

"Forget him," my father said, hardly moving.

Early the next morning as we passed back and forth in the upstairs bedroom, I hissed at Conrad, "You can't act like that. You're killing Mom."

Tying his tie in front of the speckled glass, he mocked a scornful laugh. "I'm killing her! I'm killing her! Am I the one who ruined everything for her and ruined it good? Do I sit on my ass on the front porch all day and all night? Have I gassed out on her? And you, too? Who do you think's feeding this outfit, buddy boy?"

He turned, and his lean, bitter face passed close to mine. "She's feeding this outfit, out of her little old sock."

I swallowed.

"Do you think he'll ever do anything again? He's lost his pride. Do you think he'll ever face up to that?"

I hesitated.

"Do you? All right. Tell me. Do you? Say it. Do you think he'll ever face up to that and get off his can?"

"Yes," I said. "Yes, I do."

"Ha. Ha," he said, rolling up his shirt sleeves two turns. "Ha. Ha. Ha. Ha. Ha."

I felt sick with confusion.

"Where — where're you working?"

"At the Chinaman's, buddy." He was going out the door. "I wash the dishes. I told him I had experience."

I nodded.

"My pride doesn't bother me half as much as my stomach."

"Yeh."

168

Then he was gone. I listened to his heels on the stairs, across the lower floor, the slam, and silence.

I sat down heavily on the edge of the bed. Inside my brain nothing went from one point to another. It was a dark warren with all the passages blocked, and my mind ran from one to the next, scratching to get through.

After a while, a long while, I don't know how long, I went downstairs and outside and past my mother sitting on the back stoop and into the little garage and pulled down some planks that were stored on the rafters.

While my mother watched from the stoop, I nailed together some posts and planks, shattering several hammerstones, into a kind of sofastead and carried it into the house. I spread the soogans from my bedroll over it. For a picture I found my calendar copy of Charlie Russell's "Last of the 5,000." It was supposed to be Charlie Russell's first painting, dashed off once when he was marooned in a cow camp in the midst of a blizzard. The owners of the outfit sent a message through, inquiring how the boys were doing, and for reply Charlie had drawn his picture of a lone steer standing against the snowy blast.

"That's us," I thought and tacked it over the couch. Then into a blue Mason jar from the fruit cellar I stuffed a branch of sagebrush and sprinkled its drying silvery leaves with water until it gave off its pungent prairie fragrance which I inhaled, suddenly thinking, if Conrad got work washing dishes, there must be something in this town, I went out the front door, past my father tipped back in the oak chair, and down the steps, and headed downtown.

As I passed the bank, I saw the tan shades drawn at the window, the black and gilt letters wearing away, the

flanking classical pilasters guarding the emptiness inside. Across the street on the veranda of the Laurel the
manager sat in one hickory rocker, leaning sideways,
and made confab with the solitary drummer rocking beside him, his knees spread apart, his three-inch yellow
suspenders holding his pants up over his belly. I didn't
stop, cut across the hot street and around the next
corner to Mr. Goldstein's. I tried the door handle and
couldn't make it give. I rattled the door, but it didn't
rattle much. The safety lock was on inside. Then I
pressed my face to the window and cupped my hands
against my temples and waited to see the dim interior.
After a minute I saw the counters covered with sheets
and beyond them, in back, the bench where Mr. Goldstein had worked on his agates. The bench was bare. No
tools, no grinding machine, no clutter and mess. Mr.
Goldstein had packed up and left. No wonder I hadn't
seen Sonny since school let out. He could have said good-
by. I went back to the corner and stood there with my
fingers stuck in my hip pockets. The doors to the saddlery stood open, and I looked the other way. Somebody
went into the Plainsman. The bars did steady business,
and so did Mae Flanagan's, but I was too young and too
scared for either of them. Then there were the garages
and gas stations, cafes like the Chinaman's, the shops,
but they were no use. I swung around the block to the
Delaney garage. In the showroom a new truck, a pickup,
stood by itself behind the big glass windows. No one was
around, and I opened the door into the shop. It was
high and dark and cool, and except for the thick greasy
smell it would have been pleasant. Two cars were jacked
up, and a third was raised on a grease rack.

"Howdy, Pistol."

I grinned all over. "Howdy, Texas. For cri yi, what are you doing here?"

"I'm workin'," he said. He stood up and wiped his hands on a grease rag. "I come into town to seek my fortune, Pistol." His white forehead gleamed above his tanned cheeks, and his hair was forever matted flat and dank from long years under a sweaty hat.

"But I can't hardly breathe in here. Soon's I can, I'm goin' to get away from this town. I'm goin' to ride for those piny hills where I got some room. Why, a man can't hardly stretch out in this place."

I laughed, and we shook hands, while I was thinking that with any luck I'd be on hand the day he couldn't stand it any longer, and if I had first place in line, maybe I could get his job.

Crossing Main Street again, going past the Laurel where the manager and the drummer still rocked on the veranda, I went down the basement steps into the newspaper building where Richie Greatbear bundled papers. After I gave him my paper route, Richie had stayed with it and now he managed circulation. That is, he dealt papers to the little kids and took their money and kept their accounts. He offered me the makings, and we rolled and puffed.

"Doing the rounds?" Richie said. "No luck?"

"No luck." We puffed in silence.

"Sonny's gone," I said. Bear stared at me.

"How do you know that?"

I told him, and he said, "That's a hell of a note. He could have said something."

"Maybe too hard to explain," I said.

We fell silent again, and I scratched a stove match along my Levi's and lit the stump of my cigarette. Richie pulled out a bottom desk drawer, and we propped our feet on it.

"Been out to the reservation?" I asked, and Richie pushed the papers on the desk and shook his head, "I don't go out there anymore." Surprised, I waited. "You can't live in two places, out there and in here. Hell, it rips you to pieces."

"I thought you loved it out there. It always sounded like it when you talked about it."

"I did, I did, when I was a kid. There isn't any better life. Everybody's got a pony and all that open space to fool around in and the elders taking care of everybody and deciding the business of the tribe and some old geezer telling the old stories at night. It was great, it couldn't have been greater until one day I really saw it. My grandmother was sick. She died later. A lot of them were sick and poor, so poor it'd make you sick to see it, and the elders deciding from the old ways that didn't even have a reason to exist anymore. And the stories were always old. There weren't any new ones because nothing new happens."

"You sound kind of mad about it."

His voice moderated right away. "I'm not really mad, but cripes, you should try it, Cat. There's one guy my age who keeps asking me, should I cut my braids off? Every time he sees me, I can feel him looking at my ears and the back of my head. I can feel him thinking all over my head," and he laughed with a touch of his old affection. "I feel kind of sorry for him. It's scary to cut your braids off. You wouldn't understand, I guess, what that would mean to a reservation kid."

Puffing, I said, "I guess I wouldn't really. Maybe it would be like making up my mind to leave town,"

and Bear looked surprised, and asked, "Are you thinking of lighting out?"

"No, of course not, I don't know what made me think
of that, just an example, I guess."

"I guess I've lit out, at least, I think I have," and
Richie pulled his Bull Durham out of his breast pocket
and rolled another damp, twisted cigarette. "You can't
go back and forth from here out there. You can't run
that fast," and Bear laughed. "My grandmother said
that once when I was sitting with her during her sick-
ness, and I told her I was trying to decide something,
figure out a life for myself, and she said, Grandson, first
you must decide if you are a white man or an Indian.
You can't run fast enough to be both. That really set me
thinking."

In the cool dim basement we sat in thought for a
while, the smoke thickening. I blew smoke through my
nose and let what Richie said hit the backplate of my
mind and rattle around.

Bear laughed his free, easy laugh. "Here comes my
white tribe now." Through the open door tumbled the
first couple of paper boys.

Halfway across the backyard I heard my mother
shriek, "Where have you been? Run down to the Chinaman's. Conrad got his old job back and he's gone out to
Kincaid's. Hurry, run, run!" And turning, I ran across
the yard, down the alley, slackening as I passed LeJoi's,
picking up speed into Main Street, across it, around to
the alley and into the cafe's back door. There over the
sink stood Raf Gomez.

"Hallo, keed," he said.

"You got here first."

"You're damn rights," he said.

I went home the front way and sat down on the top step to the porch near where my father sat in the oak kitchen chair. We said only a few words to each other, but I felt a greater community with him than I had for a long time, maybe I had never felt it before. We were a lot alike, I thought, in the same circumstance. We were together. And Conrad, he was in some other place, going it alone and always ahead.

The next morning my mother said, "Billy, we can plant a garden in the backyard. My mother always had a kitchen plot behind our house in Eau Claire."

"Let's make it big," I said.

I borrowed a shovel and turned the soil on half the backyard, and with my mother we planted beans and onions and lettuce and radishes and tomatoes and bordered them with rows of zinnias and marigold. My mother's tightened, nerve-ravaged face relaxed as we worked and discussed what would grow best and quickest and whether we liked onions boiled or creamed and how, later, we could gather the seed for next year. Several days passed before I made the rounds again.

As the summer progressed, the heat and drought destroyed what greenness the early spring had brought about. Along the gutters the dust devils whirled and spun across the streets, swaying like dervishes. People moved up and down the sidewalks, slowly, without purpose. Occasionally a truck pulled up at a corner and dropped off a cow puncher who pulled his saddle out of the back and was left standing by his gear looking off up the street. He was the lonesomest sight of all. Standing in the shade under Acton's awning, I watched him, listening all the time to what the other guys were saying.

Hack Davis said he was going to join the forestry conservation service or maybe the army. He wasn't going to hang around here with nothing doing, and we fell silent, thinking what it would be like faraway and alone, not that Hack was going to do it. He always had a plan which he never hatched. Then somebody yelled, "Here it comes!" We tumbled into Acton's drugstore and slammed the door and pressed against the glass.

Dust choked the sky, gritty, hard, sandy dust, not dust really, particles of dirt, of soil, of the prairie that once had been. It filled the street so that the buildings across the way made only vague blocks. The dust and grit rode the wind as it rose, whining and growling, and skimmed the hard, pebbly grains of dirt and dust and soil and drove them with demonic force down the street, whipping towering clouds and little funnels around the corners, between the buildings, beating like hail against the glass. A little eddy of sand came in under the door.

When it subsided and the building across the street emerged again, the street was empty and the cowboy was gone.

I made the rounds daily, looking and waiting and hoping to be at the right place when some cowboy couldn't take it anymore and headed for the wide-open spaces and the piny hills beyond, and finally, after days and weeks, I was. I stepped into the Red Crown station on the corner of Main and the highway and asked the man for a job, and he said, "Will you work evenings and Sundays?" and I said, "Sure thing," and he said, "You're on."

That night I commanded the round kitchen table, patting my mother kindly when she wept for joy, watching my father sideways but the old man didn't show much of anything before I said that now we could go back to the Safeway, and he said, "No, we don't."

"Why not? It's a lot cheaper."

"We're staying with Armand LeJoi."

"But that's stupid," I said, and my mother shrieked. I met my father's straight, bitter glare for a full minute, maybe more, trying not to blink, but I couldn't help it anymore than I could help looking away before he did, and suddenly I envied Conrad who could always stare him down, who had the gall I never would have.

By the end of the week I was just as glad Conrad was out of town when it became apparent what kind of a job I had. When I asked to be paid, the man gave me a commission, a percentage of the sales which were meager in themselves. Nights and Sundays, what were they going to add up to? He left me staring at my shoes. There wasn't anything else, and we both knew it.

To Bear and Hack and Raf I spread the word, and the guys with cars came out when they needed a dollar's worth. One pump carried fifteen cents a gallon gas that knocked like a trip-hammer in the engine, and it was a very big seller. After I measured out a dollar's worth and the car pulled away, I could hear it knocking painfully in the low gears. Most of the evening I spent polishing the bulging Red Crown and the White Crown which topped each pedestal, wiping the pumping lever, dusting the oil can rack and sweeping the platform clean of sand.

Among my steady customers for the fifteen-cent-tank was Mr. Burbank, who picked up a dollar's worth every week or so. Afterwards we leaned on his car fender and talked about the NRA and the minimum wage of thirty-five cents an hour and Norman Thomas and FDR and what he meant when he said, "My policy is as radical as American liberty, as radical as the Constitution of the United States." It was from Burbank that I first heard about the dam, the proposal for a barrier on the Missouri River so big that the reservoir behind it would send enough moisture into the air to change the climate of eastern Montana. Mr. Burbank laughed till he coughed over that one.

"Someday I hope somebody writes about this," he said, "about what it was like, how we felt, the straws we reached for."

"Who will believe it?"

"I don't know. Sometimes I hardly believe it myself."

I liked the station. The little stucco house with the red Spanish tile roof accumulated terrible heat during the day, but when I came on in the evening, the night breeze began and gently cleared the small room. I brought a washtub from home and got ice and stocked the tub with Coke which helped the trade considerably. After a little word-of-mouth advertising the station became the place to go. A Coke and a dollar's worth of gas to get you and your date into the boondocks and back — that was more interesting than the movies.

When I tended the station all day on Sundays, I had to sit outside. Tipped back in my chair, I read Dos Passos's *The 42nd Parallel*, which Burbank brought to me. It was a funny book, made up like a movie of frames and sequences, some of them right out of the newspapers and recent history, some of them fiction. I could hardly read three paragraphs without stopping to think what they made me think, about my own life, the world around me, on the 48th parallel. My mind exploded outward with every page, not knowing that my eyes watched the highway, saw the small truck careen into view. In the shimmering heat on the road at first it looked unreal. The truck swayed from side to side in an irregular rhythm. Bedsprings appeared over the cab, and a washtub bulged on the side. The whole apparition was covered with dust. Behind the windshield, cranked partly open, a man in an ancient felt hat held the wheel and beside him sat a woman in a sunbonnet. Honyockers. So the honyockers were on the move again.

The truck turned, wobbled onto the platform and clanked to a stop.

"Howdy," I said.

The man got out, saying nothing, and looked over the pumps. "That one," he said, pointing to the fifteen cents a gallon sign.

"South Dakota?" I asked, opening his tank.

He nodded, watching me sharply.

"Things pretty dry there this year?"

"Pretty dry," he said. "How about here?"

"Pretty dry," I said. "The spring was better than it has been, but lately it's burning up again."

He looked around, across the cottonwood trees, scanning the sky.

"Californie," he said, "that's where we're goin'. Californie."

I checked the tires, glancing at the woman as I went around. She stared ahead, her lips sunken and puckered, the eyes under the sunbonnet deeply shaded. I wiped the windshield in front of her, but she took no notice.

"A dollar and a half," I said.

Out of his overalls he pulled a small brown leather purse, scraped and worn, and opened its maw between his thickened fingers, and slowly, carefully, with great pain, he reached inside with thick thumb and fore-finger, and pulled out the money coin by coin.

"Thanks a lot," I grinned, calling after him, "good luck." But he paid no attention, steering the reeling truck into the highway to the terrible knocking in the motor.

When I walked home that night, the heat had not moderated very much. The breeze stirred the treetops, but the dust in the gutters lay still and the brown parched lawns gave off no odors. I passed our garden, which had been sprinkled early in the evening so that the onions and tomatoes spiced the air. I almost stepped on my mother sitting on the backsteps in the dark.

She didn't greet me, and after I said a few cheery things and fell silent, she whispered, "He's gone. Your dad, he's gone."

Chilled to the marrow, I began to stammer, "What did he say? He's probably gone somewhere, he's gone to get work, he'll come back, where did he go?"

She didn't know where he had gone. She didn't know when, nor if, he had some prospect. He had left a note, saying he was going after work and when he found it, if he found it, he would come back for us. In the mean-time, he said, Billy must take care of you.

I shivered in the stifling night. For the first time, there was no one, nothing, between me and the Arctic cold.

Final Farewells

14

From my perch at the Red Crown station I watched them, the long freight trains puffing slowly across the plain toward town. I watched the men sitting on top, half a dozen or more on each car with others sitting in the open doors, their legs dangling, one standing alone in the open boxcar urinating into the weeds. Watching, I feared them, yearned to be with them, despised them, bled for them. They tore at my imagination, making me ask where do they come from, why, whose fathers are they? The questions were bitter and unanswered.

One such man stopped by our place. He was seated on the back stoop when I came home, a plate on his knees, wiping it with chunks of bread. I brushed by him.

"He can go down to the soup kitchen," I told my mother.

"He wanted some work." She was pleading. "He weeded the garden. Your father may be somewhere . . ."

"Okay. Here's my pay."

Some nights I lay awake thinking of ways to find him, the state police, G-men, setting out myself on a long odyssey of freights and hobo jungles, and other nights I couldn't care less. To hell with him. We were eating.

A month passed, six weeks. Conrad came home from Kincaid's. Halfway up the alley he nailed me. "Where's the old man?"

"Well, he left. He went looking for work."

"Ran out, hey?"

"Well, he left a note." Why did I have to protect him? He didn't deserve it.

"So he left without telling anybody. He just ran out while nobody was around."

"He went to look for work, I told you. He said he'd be back if he found it. I mean when."

"What'd he say, if or when?"

"I think he said both."

Conrad swore bitterly at me which struck me as about what you get when you stand in the middle. "Why didn't you let me know? I could have sent home my pay. I was so damn mad at the old man for sitting on his rear on the porch that I didn't care if he starved to death." And he eyed me sourly again. "Why didn't you write?"

A funny nervousness stirred inside me. Why hadn't I told him? "You didn't write so I didn't write, I don't know, I don't think I thought of it, as a matter of fact, I've felt kind of — I can't think of the word to describe it — like I was just going through motions, not thinking about anything."

He stared at me, the sourness changing to disbelief, saying, "Oh, sure." Then, before it was too late, I remembered to keep my mouth shut with Conrad.

When Raf left the daytime shift, Conrad signed on

again at the Chinaman's cafe, washing dishes for a little change and meals, and I returned to school for the last time in my life, I figured, and I couldn't see that it had changed much. Practically everybody's dad was out of work or taking what he could get or doing his old job for greatly reduced pay. Rumors came and went that the schools were going to close, that the teachers hadn't been paid for months, but nothing happened. The hell of it was, nobody wanted them to close. All the pleasure had been drained from that boyhood dream. While the pale, early sun filtered through the dirty school windows, I talked a lot with Burbank about what he called "the political situation" and what I made sure centered in Chicago.

A killing frost sent the garden into oblivion before I had time to pick it clean. I had already buried beets and carrots under layers of sand in the cold basement, placed squash separately on planks to keep the air circulating around them, and picked endless quantities of green beans for my mother to put up. To keep off starvation I recommend green beans. They bear and bear and bear.

Weeks passed, and autumn became winter with its polar exposure, as Burbank called it. It was not the only cold element. There was Conrad. This time, in the privacy of our room, if there was any privacy in that echoing chamber, I nailed him.

"You'll kill her with silence. You'll kill everybody that way. You just come in the door and rip upstairs and change your tie and clear out again."

"What do you want me to do? I eat at the Chinaman's because that's part of my pay, and damn good thing it is, too. I bring home the rest. What more do you want?"

"Can't you see what you're doing to her? Are you blind or something?"

"Listen, buddy, what do you want me to do? What are you blaming me for? I'm doing my part."

"I know you're doing your part. That's not what I mean. She's had about all she can take. She's operating on instinct. That's about all she can do, and if she loses another pound the next wind will blow her away. What I mean is, she needs more than your pay."

"All right but lay off. I — do — not — like — it." And he flipped my tie in my face.

We gathered around the kitchen table with Conrad seating our lady mother and mocking the absent old man and my mother reprimanding him for disrespect as she put the red sock on the table and emptied its contents. I laid out my pay; Conrad spread out his; and we counted. We set aside what we needed for the rent, calculated the food cost, took a percentage of what was left for contingencies, and warned each other not to get sick or slip on the ice. Taking the rest, we walked down to the Palace to see the Marx Brothers in *Horse Feathers*. It wasn't a thoroughgoing success. Conrad and I nearly died laughing, but my mother was shocked and thought they were crude and coarse and insinuating, which was why we laughed.

Now the world outside lay dead beneath a great weight of snow which fell and filled the streets and covered the plains and fell again and rode the fifty-mile-an-hour winds up the slopes and over the gumbo humps and shoulders which rose from the white prairies.

One daybreak, just as the night began to lift, I awoke to find myself alone in the old double bed and my mother leaning over me.

"Billy," she whispered. "Billy, wake up. Wake up and get your rifle. There's an antelope in the backyard."

I leapt out of bed and pulled my gun from the closet. She held my father's bathrobe for me and knotted the sash around me as we stole to the kitchen window.

In the gray dawn I could see the graceful creature nibbling the tops of weeds and grass in the garden plot. Her rear end was turned toward me, the white rump almost shining in the coming light. Silently I opened the back door, took my stance and waited. The doe raised her head. On her slender legs the flesh was torn to ribbons where she had broken time and again through the crust of snow. Then turning slowly and easily, she offered me her flank. I raised my gun and fired. My mother slumped at the kitchen table, crying, "Oh, Billy, meat!" and weeping again.

I was hoisting the carcass to the clothesline when Conrad stalked into the yard through the snow.

"Up kind of early, aren't you?" he said.

"Dishwashing kind of late, aren't you?" I said, and we laughed. "Give me a hand."

"Okay, don't mind if I do."

Together we skinned and disemboweled it, as I had seen it done many times out at Sam's. Before we were finished, it had stiffened and begun to freeze. The carcass hung there for weeks wrapped in a sheet, because my mother couldn't bear to look at it from the kitchen window. Because of it through that bitter winter we had meat.

Under the spring winds the snowdrifts crumpled and vanished. No rain fell, and the prairie broke open in cracks and gashes.

Mother Nature, Mother Nature, I whispered, ease up a little, will you? But Mother Nature was deaf.

I studied the picture postcard that Sonny sent me, and all its glossy black and white transposed into lush green prairie grass and bare distant buttes watching and it read, Montana cattle graze along the scenic route of the Great Northern Railroad, route of the Empire Builder, or something like that and under it in Sonny's purposeful hand, he wrote, "Going to the U in Missoula. Not too bad. Girls great. Living at home. Dad okay, business likewise. Good luck to a swell guy."

Good luck to a swell guy. That's what we were writing to everybody, holding the copies of the high school annual against locker doors, passing them around in class. "I'll never forget the good old days in sophomore English." "Knowing you has been the greatest experience in my life, good luck to a swell guy." "You've got what it takes to get ahead. If anybody makes it, you will." Makes what, I wondered, but didn't ask, scrawling across Syb Stoker's, "You've got the best figure in school. Keep it up." In a space I marked, "Reserved for Raf," he wrote meticulously, "Friends are the most important thing in the world, and you are a true friend. If our friendship ever dies, I shall drive into a telephone pole going ninety miles an hour. It is no use living without friends. I hope that we meet again in later life." And across the team picture Hack Davis said, "I'll never forget the way you looked in the locker room after football practice. Good luck to a swell guy who can really take the bruises." Across one page in the back I wrote, "Reserved for the girl with the blue hair ribbon." The space was never filled.

Lying in bed and staring up at the ugly light fixture, I spent some time on late Saturday mornings thinking about Syb Stoker and wondering if I should ask her to the senior prom and if I should spend that much money on anybody, including myself, and I was thinking about her in a number of ways, she was rumored to be hotter than a pistol, when footsteps striding across the backyard alerted me. I went rigid. I listened with every inch. No ring. No knock. Just the door slamming. Shrieks. Sobs. A man's voice. I swung out of bed and hit the floor standing. It was a deeply known man's voice. I was halfway downstairs before my conscious mind said whose it was. He had come home. My father had come home.

New Promise

15

"There's plenty of work up there. How's that coffee, Mother?" He was exuberant. Not an exuberant man, he ran over with high spirits. When my mother leaned over to fill his cup, he patted her. "Work for everybody. Hard work for tough guys like you, Conrad." He laughed and pounded Conrad on the back, making him smile, grudging and rueful. "And plenty of tough guys." He looked out the window and shook his head. "Oh, my, it's good to be back."

At that Conrad and I exchanged a glance, for we were both thinking, then why didn't you write? Why didn't we hear from you? Bitterness, disillusion, new knowledge came up, I felt it, I saw it in Conrad's eyes, but the question could not be asked. It came too close to the raw heart of things, where the deep wounds lie.

"Is that where you've been all winter?"

"I got in on it early, when they needed men to clear the brush. The surveyors were hardly finished when we got going. Then later when the weather turned bad, the machines came in and did what they could do. They plan to work year round up there. It is really going to be something."

He hugged my mother again and said, "The biggest earth-filled dam in the whole world. It's going to be the biggest thing that ever happened to this country, and the best, too. It's going to turn this prairie green again." He tapped the table. "And soon, too. They expect six — seven thousand men to hire out up there this summer. Men from all over, back East, California, everywhere, but mostly from right here. It's going to be a dam for Montana built by Montanans."

"Where'd Montana get the bucks for anything like that?" Conrad asked.

Exasperation edged his voice, when my father replied, "It's a federal project, Conrad. FDR knows what we need out here. He has the little man at heart."

"Especially the little man who votes Democratic," Conrad said.

"Which is about everybody so don't sound so cynical," I said.

"Then there are going to be lots of dams in this country."

"Well, okay, maybe we need them, the way Dad says."

To that Conrad didn't reply and gave me a long despising look as if to say, whose side are you on, buddy?

"The government's putting up a whole town, houses, a hospital, the whole works. That's FDR for you. But it's a town for men, the dam workers. Mostly men, you see, will come and leave their families back home. But I can't take that anymore. I've been wracking my brains to think of some way to have you with me, and now now . . ."

In the seconds it took him to push back his plate and cup and saucer and set the unused silver aside I glanced around the kitchen table. My mother looked almost relaxed, almost joyful, her uncombed hair still frowzy from sleep. Conrad sat back, his chin down so that he looked across the table through half lowered lids and twiddled with his spoon while he waited. Between my mother and Conrad I sat and I wondered how I looked, and wondering I rubbed my chest with a handful of faded pajamas.

Sensing the drama, my father waited, looked around a moment longer, rubbed his hands. "Now, now," leaning forward, "this is what I have in mind. Now I want you boys to say what you think." I felt uneasy. Never in my life had I heard him say he cared what any of us thought or had he ever acted like it, but maybe he had changed. I waited.

"The thing for us to do is pack up what we have here, if we want it and Lord knows there isn't much to want," laughing, "and get on up to the damsite. If we get going right away, we'll be there before everybody in the whole state gets there. We'll get in on the ground floor, before it gets big and it's going to be big, no doubt about that. I'll let you in on a little secret," motioning us forward. Only Conrad held back, conscious and stubborn with his arms crossed like a barrier. "I'm dickering for a little property up there. That's right. Not too far from the dam. There's nothing on it now. I couldn't buy it if there was, but when things start to sprout the way I think they're going to, that little patch can't miss." I sat back and folded my arms, not thinking exactly, a thun derhead of past experience mounting in my head. My mother seemed to shrivel before my eyes. "Now — now, don't get excited."

"Who's excited?" Conrad said.

"What's the matter with all of you? You two — don't you have any adventure in you? You going to stick around and hoe the pea patch all your lives? I know Conrad's got a lot of pea patch in him for all his tough guy business, but you, Billy, I thought you'd be all for it. You've always been a great one for leaving home. Why, when you were a little kid, Mother used to call me at work every day or so to tell me you were lost again, you'd run off without your leggings on. You were always the adventurous one. Now what's the matter with you?"

I stirred uneasily, feeling trapped like a criminal guilty of a crime but not the one he is accused of. "Well, I don't know, I just don't know enough about it. I've got work here, and I don't know." Conrad was watching me. "I don't just want to quit with nothing else in sight, I mean . . ."

"I've told you, there is plenty of work up there. There is work for everybody. I can guarantee it. Don't you believe me?"

"Frankly, no," Conrad said.

My father's lips twitched, showing the edge of his upper teeth, and to stop them he squeezed them together in a rigid line.

"I was going out to Kincaid's soon as they start hiring for the summer. I hadn't figured on anything else. One thing for sure, I am sick as hell of dishwashing, and I don't want to do it here or any place else, even on the biggest earth-filled dam in the whole damn world."

"I'm not talking about dishwashing. I'm talking about man-sized jobs. Man-sized."

"The dam sounds pretty good," I murmured.

My father ignored me and addressed Conrad, "You're practically a man. In lots of ways you are a man. You've got to make your own decision, and I'm not trying to make it for you. I couldn't if I tried. All I'm asking is, look at the proposition. Look at it as though somebody else told you about it, not me."

My mother made a little cry, and suddenly I looked at her, but more than that, I suddenly thought of her, saw her. For all my father's patting her and hugging her and calling for coffee, not once had he asked her if she wanted to go. Did she want to pack up everything, such as it was, and take herself on to a new site, someplace she had never been before, where few people had, and one where even the government didn't expect many women? What would she do, how would she live, a wispy frail woman placed upright on the naked plain? Oh, my God. I groaned inside, we've consulted her not once, not once. She stared straight ahead, the milky coffee turning cold in her cup. We herded her like cattle. With terrible clarity I saw her, small and thin, almost a skeleton, the nerve-ravaged face, the hands scrubbed white and raw. What did she think? What did she feel? We didn't know. Even my father, he didn't know. Did we even care? My heart contracted. For years we had thundered through the house, eating like horses, wanting, expecting, getting. I turned and put my arm along the back of her chair, and I saw her eyes a faded blue, childishly innocent and numbed as if they asked from a distance of decades, what happened?

"Mom, how about you, Mom? What do you want to do?"

She smiled at me, her little chin-up smile.

"Just so there's a roof over our heads," she said.

I felt like a murderer.

Paying no attention, my father was going on, "You don't have to decide right away. But you've got to make up your mind pretty quick. We can't wait all summer or it will be too late. Not for the jobs, but too late for — " and his voice petered out.

I followed Conrad down the back stoop into the yard, wanting to ask him questions, wanting to know, "What do you think? Do you think you'll — it's — ?" and following him across the broken clods of last summer's garden.

"You'd better hoe your pea patch," he said.

"Only if I'm here to reap," I said. "That's a quote from the Bible."

"How do you know?"

"I get around."

"Some of the places you hang out will do you no good."

"What do you think, Conrad?"

"How can I know yet? Kincaid's is where I want to go, that much is certain." He glared at me fiercely. "I'm not like him," and he jerked his thumb over his shoulder. "I'm not going to be like him. I'm not going to run all over the map chasing butterflies. If this prairie ever greens up and it'll take more than one world's greatest earth-filled dam to do it, I'm going to get myself a little piece, near a river, a piece that nobody can get away from me and the sun can't burn it up and I can live on it, and I'm going to stay there and hoe my pea patch, God dammit, and be satisfied for the rest of my life."

Following him down the alley, I nodded, "What'll you do then? I mean now? Between now and when you get this little piece of green prairie?"

"Keep my eye out for Jim Kincaid."

"Where are you going?"

"The Chinaman is going to tell me when Jim comes in."

"He's sure to go in there," I nodded. "I'll go downtown with you."

"You're in your pajamas, and your barn door's open."

"Oh. Yeah. Well, I guess I'll go down later." Pulling my pajamas together, I ran back to the house. Suddenly I wanted to talk with Richie. Bear would listen, Bear knew how to keep his mouth shut; and he had already made the big decision in his life, to be a white man and live in the white man's world. He had broken with his past life, or a part of his past where it was safe. Now I faced the break. Time ran away behind me, taking everything with it while I was propelled forward. The only thing that stood still and made me feel good was that I knew the place where I was. I knew it forwards and backwards, down to its guts and up to its sky. I knew it, that was all, which was everything.

In the basement of the *Star* building I found Hack Davis sitting at Richie's desk.

"Hi," he said.

"Hi." I stared at him while he shuffled papers. Finally I asked, "Richie around?" although I knew the answer.

"Richie's gone back to the reservation."

Hack needed a job. Hack's father owned the paper,

and he gave Hack a job. That job belonged to somebody else, a longtime buddy, but — well, times are tough, kid. Hack couldn't look at me. I didn't much want to look at him.

Outside the light blinded me. I stood blinking at the top of the concrete stairs and thinking, so — and wandered to the corner where I stood with my fingers stuck into my hip pockets, surveying Main Street.

"Tom! Tom!" I ran toward the Plainsman. "Driscoll! Tom!" Tom stopped with his hand on the door, looking blankly my way.

"Howdy, Pistol."

"How's everything? How's Punkin Crick?"

"I dunno, Pistol."

"Aren't you out there?"

"Not at the present time," Tom said.

Before the silence lengthened, I hurried on, "I'm thinking of going up to the new dam. My dad wants us all to go, but I've got a job here, not much but something, and . . ."

Tom nodded. "I heard about the dam." He pulled his hand from his pocket and examined his change.

"What do you think about it, Tom, going up there and everything?"

He closed his hand on his coins. "Well, it's one way, I guess, Pistol. Wanna beer?"

"No, thanks, Tom, Horace won't let me in, anyway."

"I'll be seein' ya, Pistol."

"Sure thing, Tom."

Once again I stood alone looking up Main Street. I walked past the Chinaman's where Conrad waited over the sink for Jim Kincaid and crossed over to Acton's and stood under the awning, thinking of an ice-cold ingot of cherry Coke spreading out in the pit of my stomach when Burbank came along the sidewalk. His curled up smile opened when he saw me.

"How's it going, Bill? Come and have a Coke with me."

Seated on the stools at Acton's fountain, we tossed the odds and ends back and forth while the soda jerk with a cauliflower ear squirted fine streams of fizz into glasses. Into my straw I said, "My dad came home." I didn't expect it to be so hard to say.

"I was sure he would, Bill."

"I wasn't, well, sometimes I wasn't, sometimes I was. Now he wants us to go with him up to the dam, the big dam on the Missouri, the one that's supposed to change the climate. They really are building it."

He nodded. "I doubt if it will change the climate, but there will be other benefits. Work, for one thing."

"That's what he says. He thinks it'll be a big thing, and he'll have another chance for something big like the horsemeat plant. I don't think my mother could take one more of those. I don't know if I can. Not that we've got anything left to lose. What's the matter with just living, anyway? Taking what you've got and — and being happy? What's the good of chasing after something better and bigger all the time? Mostly it's a mirage, anyway. They don't strike it rich in the next town."

Burbank nodded. "No, they don't, not many, but it's a compelling vision nevertheless, and it comes true just often enough to stay alive in every one of us." He laughed. "You know, I was cleaned out in the crash of '29. I was a ridiculous, underpaid schoolteacher in the bowels of Chicago. I had invested all I had, five hundred dollars which was my all, my everything. What business

195

does a schoolteacher have investing on the stock market? What business does anyone with resources limited to five hundred dollars? I never asked myself those questions. Oh, I did a little, way in the back of my head, and I paid no attention and invested my life savings. I wasn't the only one. Half the teachers at Nicholas Senn played the market. They had brokers. Talk about illusions! Well, it will be a long cold winter before they have dreams like that again. What a nightmare." He finished his drink, and we moved to the brilliant doorway.

"Maybe that's more of a delusion."

"You're right. Good point, Bill. You know, however, about illusions, Wordsworth thought that they were very important to youth, that they even aided in the process of development."

"Mr. Burbank, that's what worries me most, that I'll spend my whole life chasing after something that never comes true, that probably isn't even there. Can't you live just taking the whole thing straight on? Without dreaming up something or getting drunk so you can stand it?"

"It's possible, Bill, but it really takes guts to live that way, looking the whole naked business square in the eye." He held out his hand. "Good luck, Bill. Very best of luck."

I turned toward home. I guessed I'd go to the dam. What was the harm in just going up there, seeing what it was like? The dam wouldn't last forever, only the years it took to build it, and then the jobs would be gone, and the little towns, the crop of houses my father described, would be gone, and the men who came to live and work there would drift on. Behind the dam the water would accumulate. The great Missouri would back up behind the barrier and spread out, filling a lake, seeping into the parched and stony soil which cried out for moisture. Just to go look, see it, maybe work there awhile, what was the harm in it? Maybe Conrad made too big a thing of the whole affair. It wasn't the last decision before closing time. He wasn't going to wash dishes in the Chinaman's for the rest of his life anymore than I would pump Red Crown gas for the rest of my natural life, and the old man would not work on the dam. We needed something to tide us over until things straightened out a bit. If they never did, well, then, we could work on that later when we knew for sure. Just do it for now. Of course, my father couldn't do it that way. He had to have a little dream, a little piece of land, a horsemeat plant, a carload of binoculars, something to run after. That was the way he was. But you didn't have to be that way. You could look the whole naked business straight in the eye. I burst out laughing. Burbank was a funny guy. But what was the use of deciding? Richie decided and got his decision reversed for him. As long as there really was work on the dam, as long as I didn't give up what little I had for nothing, there wasn't much use my hanging around.

When I got home, Conrad was in the bedroom packing his duffle.

"Kincaid's isn't hiring," he said.

Deal

16

That night we packed a borrowed truck, loaded it with the meager household goods, the clothing in cardboard boxes, the last of the wrinkled carrots, the couch of boards and soogans. With a shoe box of blue envelopes under my arm I passed my mother stuffing the red rock into her battered brown leather pocketbook.

"We won't need that anymore," I said.

"We can't be sure, Billy," she said. After her death decades later I found the sock in her dresser drawer. Three hundred dollars was in it.

"What's the shoe box?" Conrad said.

"Personal memorabilia."

"Forget it," he said.

Early the next morning, my mother and father in the cab, Conrad stretched out on the couch, me sitting where the tail gate went, my legs dangling, we headed north. We crossed the Yellowstone, the road rising with the land away from the joining of the two rivers and running through sheep country where the grass was cropped to the ground, the roots pulled, so that the brown stubble lay in patches with hard, dry earth between. On the brow of a passing hill stood a sheepherder's wagon, tongue down in the stubble.

Toward noon we passed over the central plateau and began the long descent to the Missouri River. Standing up and looking over the cab, we could see it making its long, sluggish meanders northeastward across the plain. In spite of the water's nearness the prairies were as scorched and desiccated as those we left behind, and the brushy sand bottoms and cottonwood groves along the banks showed edges and severed oxbows where the water no longer reached and starvation had set in.

" 'The Promised Land,' " Conrad said. "Oh, Jesus."

But it was! It was! Work, food, a new place, what other promises were there? The rest was up to us, and I pressed my fist to my mouth to hide my excitement.

We came down a long hill. At the foot of this gradual decline a town spread out before us. Not a town by any exact definition but a habitation, a collection of dwellings of such impermanence that they resembled a mining camp of the Eighties staked out on the mother lode. The long decline flattened under this scattering, supported it, and emerged beyond it in the broadest, flattest, most barren plain I had ever seen. Not a tree grew anywhere. I stared at this place over the truck side, and Conrad stood beside me and stared also.

In the distance a great dust cloud obscured part of the horizon. Where the dam was, I supposed, as we rattled into the town.

Dirt ways had been worn in every direction, any direction, wherever anybody wanted one, and along them men had pitched tents, parked gypsy wagons, covered pickups, farm trucks outfitted like prairie schooners.

The highway became the main street, wide and hot and dusty, and on each side buildings were going up. Floors were laid and the studs were up, skeletons on platforms. A long, low building was finished with a boardwalk out in front and a covered veranda for shade and big double doors wide open, and along the false front above the veranda a gaudy sign invited BRING 'ER INN. Through the big open double doors noise emptied into the street. We went on, down a row of look-alike tarpaper shanties, and in front of one, my father stopped.

There was dead silence.

Then my mother cried, "But you said it was just as good . . ." and her voice disappeared.

Conrad and I stared over the truck's side.

The door slammed.

"I said almost." My father appeared at the back, his face grim and set.

"Okay, boys, we'll unload." He went up to the front door to unlock it. When he came back to the cab door, he said, "We have electricity and running water, Mother. We're lucky," and he opened the door. She stepped out and stood there without moving. She seemed to have shrunk on the journey. She was thin to the point of wispiness, her dress flapped too loosely in the dry west wind. She even looked shorter than before. She lifted her chin and gave me her little smile which was meant to conceal all under cover of bravery. Then she walked slowly to the door. As if a signal had been given, we began to unload.

The front door of the tarpaper house opened into the kitchen. There wasn't a living room or a front room, just the kitchen which wasn't very big, with a bedroom divided from it by a beaver board partition, but there was a sink with dripping faucets and light bulbs dangling on black cords in each room. My father repeated with grim cheer. "We have electricity and running water which is more than most of the lots around here."

"We're lucky," Conrad said.

The outhouse was in back.

Into the silence my father said, "All right. Maybe I was wrong. I may have been all wet to bring you up here. I've been here all winter, trying to get the money together to get somewhere again, and it turned out to take longer than I hoped. This isn't final. We know that. I couldn't stand it alone any longer. That's all there is to it. I couldn't face it without you. It's as simple as that."

He turned his back on us, Conrad and me settling the kitchen table into place, filling half the kitchen. My mother stood still, trembling.

"I left Great Plain for this." She turned on him. "How can I go out? How am I going to take care of us?"

My father swung around. "It isn't that bad, Adelaide. You'll see. The general store is open. It's only two blocks away."

"Two blocks! Past all those gypsy wagons and those rough men!"

"All right. Don't go out then. I'll stop on my way home. Or the boys can. One of them."

I looked at Conrad, who looked at my father.

"Got any better ideas?" His glare swung over us.

No one spoke. We shifted, breathed. We were caught between a rock and a hard place.

Behind the shack halfway to the outhouse Conrad and I staked out places for our bedrolls. There wasn't room for us inside, and, anyway, it was too hot. The best thing about that little house was that the breeze blew through it without much interference.

"Conrad," I whispered as we chucked stones out of the way, "how about that Bring 'Er Inn?" I watched for his scorn, but he only laughed. "How about going over there tonight?"

"I'm with you, buddy, soon's it's dark."

After nightfall fires sparked the plain, lighting up the side of a panel truck, revealing the silhouette of squatting figures, and the scent of meat frying drifted on the wind. Conrad and I made our way to the main drag.

The wariness of an animal pulsed through me. I could feel my resources a hair trigger away. We stayed on the other side from the Bring 'Er Inn, walking shoulder to shoulder and keeping ample room between us and the action. Two bullock trains could pass abreast in that street, like all the main streets of that region which dated from way back, although no bullock trains would ever arrive here on this street built day before yesterday or possibly just yesterday. It was unpaved, just dirt and dust, and if it ever rained, mud like nothing you ever saw before, and only the boardwalks and platforms would keep you from sinking in to your boot tops. Across the street we stopped and looked through the double doors of the saloon into the bright, vibrating interior of the Bring 'Er Inn. Up and down the street men moved, dirty men, clean-shaven men, drunk and sober and in between, big and little, in overalls and

Levi's and city suits, and we moved with them, past them. Where somebody had put up a floodlight and a crew worked at hammering walls and roof into place, we stopped and watched. Where the walls and roof weren't up yet but the bar was serving a crowd and the Negro on the honky-tonk piano plinked out the beat, we stopped and watched there. We prowled the boardwalk from one end to the other.

"Jeese, I'm scared to go in the place." Conrad laughed, his nostrils flaring in and out, making me think of Sundance when we rode out early and he caught the first fresh scents on the morning wind.

"I'll bet the mining camps started up like this," I said, "out of nowhere as soon as the miners gathered on a vein and had nuggets and no place to go."

Conrad broke out laughing. "Come on, buddy."

Shoulder to shoulder in lock step we paced the boardwalk until we were opposite the Bring 'Er Inn, pivoted to face the open double doors, strode across the street straight through the entrance to the back bar and turned, putting our elbows on the counter behind us and hooking one boot heel over the brass rail. To my surprise no one particularly noticed us. I had never felt so conspicuous in my life.

The noise beat in waves. Along every wall ran a bar with a brass footrail which was lined with men, and behind the counters the bartenders worked, grinning, pulling the spigots of beer, sliding a dime off the bar, ringing the cash register next to the card CREDIT MAKES ENEMIES, LET'S BE FRIENDS. On a railed-off stand in the corner the band struck up, and the sax, accordion, violin, banjo and piano wailed "Nobody's Sweetheart Now." On the railing a bowl had been placed with a sign FEED THE KITTY, and I wondered if they played for free. A pair of swinging doors shielded a second room. In a sudden stillness I heard the chips chinking and the clicky-click of the wheel spinning. All around us men swarmed. Men in caps with bills, men in fedoras, men in suits and torn and soiled jackets, dirt stiffs — the shovel crews — with their pants rolled up above their boots and their sleeves rolled up over their biceps which were impressive, men in wide belts with pants flapping down over their heels and almost covering the toes of their shoes. God, it was a gold rush, not for bonanza, not to strike it rich, only to strike something.

"What'll you have, boys?" the bartender said.

Conrad ordered a beer, and I said, nothing. The man put both fists on the bar. "I said, what'll you have, kid, not if."

"Beer. A beer."

"I don't know which side to watch," Conrad whispered, "in front or in back."

"This bartender makes me a little nervous." I closed my hand tight around the mug handle, thinking, one bang on the bar and I'd have a weapon, and watching the tall, blond bouncer carry a man toward the door by one bicep while blood trickled down the man's neck. "Throw him out," the man yelled, cussing, "he started it."

"I would, chum, but he ain't bleedin'."

"Let's go," I said to Conrad. "You were right before we came in here. You should be scared."

"Maybe we can find a nice tea room," Conrad said.

"This place is going to be the toughest town Montana has ever seen," I said, keeping my eyes moving as we strode along the boardwalk. "This one is quieter."

We surveyed the interior of The Green Frog. The walls that were up were painted dull dark green with spots. A piano player held down an upright, and only one cowboy and a lanky city man conversed from stools at the bar. They stopped and watched us come in, listened while we ordered two beers, and finally the lanky one rose to his full height, which was around six feet four inches, and said, "Welcome to The Green Frog, gentlemen. I'm Doc Stengel. I dispense Band-Aids at the government hospital. This is John behind the mahogany." It was linoleum. "And this gentleman here has played cowboy all over Oklahoma." He stepped backward suddenly, righted his skinny frame, and belched with his chinless chin pressed into his neck.

Hesitating and wary, we introduced ourselves.

"Just get in?"

Before I could answer, I saw the cowboy's mouth drop open, heard the piano player slowing on the keyboard and the tinny tune fading away. I swung toward the door, at the ready.

Two men had entered The Green Frog and stood in the doorway. Their clothes were covered with dust, their caps caked with soil and sweat. Under their sunburns they were chalk-white in the unrelieved light of bare bulbs. They staggered to the bar. John poured out two shots of whisky before they said a word.

"What's the matter?" I asked of anyone.

One man turned to me, but he couldn't speak. His pale, cracked lips moved and stuck on his dry teeth. The other tossed down his whisky with a practiced snap, and said, "Landslide."

"Behind the dam?" John said.

The articulate man nodded. "He was driving one cat,

and I was on another, and this other guy was on a third
one close to the embankment. I heard something, I
guess, and I looked up and saw it coming and yelled and
waved, and he heard me and jumped. Two seconds later
his cat was covered up, buried, you couldn't see a corner
of it."

"What about the other guy?"

The man snapped down another shot.

"He's a goner, cat and all."

In the silence that followed the man unable to speak
put his head on the bar and slowly slid to the floor.

"First customer you've had pass out without a drink,
John," Doc Stengel said. "I'll get my tool kit."

We laughed that hysterical laughter that is like re-
covering your breath after a punch in the stomach while
the piano player struck up "The Worms Crawl In" and
Doc Stengel brought the man around.

When, late that night, I stretched out on top of my
soogans face up to the vast, familiar, star-sparkling sky,
Conrad said, "I've never seen anything like it, and I've
been in some tough joints."

"One thing for certain," I said, "this is no place for
Mom. God, this is terrible."

"The old man was out of his nut to bring her up here.
If it was just us, we could have a big time. Who cares
what a couple of young bucks do?"

"But it isn't just us."

"For two bits I'd pack her up in the truck and take
her back tomorrow," Conrad said. "She doesn't belong
here. It's bad in Great Plain but not this bad. And he
can limp along any way he can."

"Maybe she doesn't want to leave him."

"Are you crazy? She's in her right mind."

"She's kind of a little kid, though."

"She should give him a swift kick in the butt."

"Yeah, well, she should but she won't. Anyway the one thing I know for sure is that I don't want to herd her around. She's had enough of that from him and from you and me, too. It makes me kind of sick to think of it. She's sort of a little kid, but she's not a critter. If we're mad about what he's doing to her, she feels something, too. She's not a lump. She's hanging on for dear life. What if we barged in and did something we thought was right and busted up the very thing she's hanging on to?"

After some silence Conrad said, "Yeah, maybe you're right. What do we know about them, anyway?"

"Not very much. This is what really socks me, that we don't know much of anything about our own folks. We don't even see them very well. They're just around."

"Boy, I can see the old man this minute, red in the face and yelling, 'You're not going out for football. Your duty is where I need you, and I need you in the wool house.' So he wouldn't have to hire a grown man at man's wages. I can see him pretty damn well."

"I can even see him that night, but they sort of move in and out, you know what I mean?"

"All right then, you think of something. How are you going to get him to take her back to Great Plain? How are you going to get him to face up? He's making money and he's dickering on a piece of property. He'll say things are better."

"I don't know. Maybe just keep bringing it up."

Conrad hissed. "You're working against a lifetime habit, buddy, remember that."

"We can think of something. Let's give it twenty-four hours. We'll have cased the place by then, and we won't be going off half-cocked. We'll have the facts."

"All right, twenty-four hours. Then how about hitching over to the dam first thing?"

"First thing."

Twenty-four Hours
and After

17

From where we stood the far bluff of the Missouri rose
in the early mist four miles away. The dam was to
stretch from the bluff under our feet to the distant bluff
and fill the cavity between them almost level. It was
maybe a hundred yards down to the river bottom. It
would take a very wide barrier to hold back all that
water. The enormous vacancy was to hold the largest,
longest, biggest earth-filled dam in the whole world.
Already the flow had been diverted, the great fill begun.
Below us in the stream bed men drove the largest
machinery I had ever seen which crawled backwards and
forwards on caterpillar treads. I wondered where the
landslide occurred. There was no sign of it left and no
sign that it had slowed the work for an hour.

My father was right. Work was there for the asking,

but you had to have the right answer. Conrad worked up in line to the employment shack and came away a dirt stiff, report tomorrow morning, and he laced me, "What's the matter? You scared or something? Think of the pay, buddy boy, we came here for the pay."

"Maybe we won't be staying."

"Just see if you can get it. You don't have to show up."

I got in line, worked up to the window where the man asked me if I was head of a household, and I said, "Huh? I'll be eighteen . . ." But he cut me off, "Sorry, kid, step aside."

"What'd you tell the truth for, you dumb cluck?"

I shrugged, not knowing myself.

"Hey, kid," somebody in the line grabbed my shoulder and jerked his head toward the shack. "He wants you."

The man stuck his head out the window and shouted at me, "Balster is hiring in shacktown. Balster Merc. Look for it. The place isn't finished yet." Everybody laughed, and I nodded and grinned.

"You can get on later, if we stay," Conrad said. Every few minutes a truck pulled up, emptying a man or men into the line. The dust rose and drifted on the wind. The heat rose. The sun moved higher.

Shacktown had grown in the few hours it had taken us to hitch to the dam and back. Now a sign stood out: YOU ARE ENTERING THE MAIN STREET OF DEAL. Not New Deal or Square Deal or Raw Deal, just Deal, buddy, I don't like the cards I got. You could tell the newcomers. They stood on the edge of the boardwalks and looked up and down, the way we did yesterday, and we laughed at them for not knowing the ropes. I dropped off in front of the Balster Mercantile Company where two men juggled a piece of plate glass into position to cover the display window which was already displaying goods, a myriad sampling of what the general store offered inside. Only there was no inside properly speaking. I could see through from the street to the back of the store where two trucks had backed up, one unloading lumber, the other merchandise. I leaned against a post and considered and then moved across the two-bullock-trains-abreast street and sat on the edge of the boardwalk, rolled a cowboy cigarette and considered further.

Outside of the Bring 'Er Inn where the gaudy sign was all but invisible against the blinding daylight, the Balster Mercantile Company occupied the largest portion of the main drag. According to its windows, and according to all the mercs I ever knew or heard of, it sold everything. Men's work clothes, dress suits with nipped waists, Stetsons, fedoras, engineers' caps, enameled pots and pans and basins, Sterno stoves and black iron Dutch ovens, a sign reading YES, WE HAVE TENTS, every conceivable item were jumbled together in the windows along with the shoes. The shoes arrested me. In the window there were work shoes, safety boots, high-lace dress shoes, low-cut oxfords of a yellow tinge, a sturdy model with a moccasin toe. They decorated one side, and arrayed opposite them stood women's shoes in black patent leather and gleaming white, navy blue with rhinestone bows and one little strap over the heel. Tucked in a far corner were several pairs of heavy flat-heeled shoes that looked like something for nurses or honyocker women. Where were the women to wear those shoes? It set me wondering.

In the middle of the display, placed on a paper-wrapped pedestal stood a pair of cowboy boots. They were higher than those a working puncher would wear, higher heels, higher uppers, and they were polished to a glittering black and decorated from ankle to top with magnificent yellow butterflies. Just seeing them stirred my mind and made me feel good, and I thought, oh, what the hell, if you don't get on a bucker, you never know if you can ride him. You don't have to take it, and maybe there isn't anything, anyway, and I crossed the street, dodged the two workmen, and went inside, under the roof.

The man in his shirt sleeves with pencils in the breast pocket and a tailor-made behind his ear was obviously in charge, pointing here and there and yelling, "Put 'er there. No! No! No!" Swearing a blue streak, "I said there."

"Mr. Balster."

"Yeah." He glanced around and was off again. I followed behind.

"Mr. Balster."

"What'd'ya want?"

"I'm looking for a job and I wondered. I've done a lot of selling . . ." He was swearing like a sailor until a wall was slammed up in front of him and the hammering outside drowned his voice. Then he switched back the other way, bawling at another crew.

"What'd'ya say your name was?"

I hadn't said. "Bill Catlett. I'm from Great Plain."

"Pots and pans over there."

"I wondered if you needed a clerk or anything." He was off again, cussing and ordering.

"Any experience?"

I repeated, hollering above the hammering.

"Did you say Catlett? Come back tomorrow morning eight o'clock sharp."

As far as I could tell, he never looked at me, never saw me; he knew I was there like a fly or a mosquito, an itchy shoulder blade. I wasn't even certain I was hired, stepping out onto the boardwalk again, but, if I was, then we all had work, all of us.

Crossing to the back door, I saw my mother peek out the corner of the window. She took the latch off the screen to let me in. I sat down at the kitchen table and looked at her.

"Conrad got a job at the dam."

"Oh, that will be good money."

"I found a job at the merc. I think I did. I don't know what it will pay, but . . ."

"You can bring the groceries home then. You may even get a discount."

"Yes, maybe, I don't know yet."

Twenty-four hours hadn't passed. We had cased the place, found it the roughest spot on the face of the earth with work for the asking. I watched my mother make sure the screen was locked behind me. Now she extracted my one dress shirt from the heaping wash basket and was overjoyed to have reason to iron it.

"Where did all the white shirts come from?" I asked, and she said, "Dad wears a clean one every day."

"A white shirt! To the motor pool?"

"He's the dispatcher. He likes to look spruce." Leaning over the board, pressing her weight down on the iron, she looked so worn and tired, beaten down, I was scared for a moment, but she was cheery and I felt great and the moment passed into the abyss of memory.

By eight o'clock sharp the next morning the Balster Merc was enclosed; Mr. Balster in shirt sleeves stood at the front door telling a sign painter how to paint a sign to read Balster Mercantile Company; and the sign painter knelt on the sidewalk, painting the sign and clenching his jaw muscles rhythmically. When Mr. Balster saw me, he stuck his head in the open door and hollered, "Smitty! Here's a clerk for you. In shoes."

Out of the shoe department, which was right at the door, the clerk came forward, looking me over, and he was not much older than Conrad. Round-faced, getting fat, with limp white hands and moist palms, he wasn't the kind I took to right off.

"Done any selling before?"

I nodded, not saying that I sold the Great Plain *Star*, *Liberty* magazine and Red Crown gas and stood on the fringes at the sale of cattle, adding, "But not shoes."

"One guy can't keep up with the trade in here. I've been telling that to Balster for a week now."

"How long have you been here?"

"Two weeks, and I've been busier than a one-armed paper hanger. One guy can't keep up, is what I told him. I don't know how come they wear out their shoes." He laughed in long, piglike snorts. "I didn't know they were on their feet that much."

"Maybe the pressure and the heat from the engines."

He nearly split laughing. "The pressure!" he gasped. "The heat from the engines! You don't know how funny that is." He practically sobbed. "I don't mean the dam workers." He wiped his eyes between snorts. "I mean the girls."

"What girls?"

"Oh, boy, are you innocent. Are you ever innocent. Don't you know?"

"I just got here," I said angrily.

"The girls from Happy Town. Man, you ought to see them." He wet his lips. "That's where they really got the merchandise." Now rubbing his soft hands together. "Balster told me to train you," which threw him into snortling giggles and I wondered about the whole thing. "First, you got to know the stock, see? Everything we got, we got one of out. The sizes are on the boxes, see? I been here two weeks and I finally got it all memorized. It's not easy."

The customers drifted in. A honyocker first. I knew him from the bib-top overalls and stiff-brimmed hat and the great eyes haunted by disaster. Next, the cowboy from Oklahoma. It made me feel good when he walked in. I knew him, and a puncher is always a pleasure to see. Things were just as bad for him as for the honyocker, but in the cowboy mind and body went together in every movement. He tried on one work shoe and hobbled on one high heel, one flat one, to the mirror. When he hopped back, he muttered, "Don't know as I can stand it."

"It's only till it rains."

"You got a sense of humor, son. We're never goin' to get Oklahoma back. Them guys in Kansas took a likin' to it when it blew in."

"It's kind of dusty up here, too."

"Son, you can water the whole state of Montana with the whisky on this street."

In the background Smitty snorted out of control, snuffle-haw, snuffle-haw, snuffle-haw.

About eleven o'clock we were lounging against the table edge when I saw her hesitate in the open doorway. Against the brilliant light of the street I could see the outline of her thighs through her skirt. A huge hat darkened her face, and all I could tell, looking into the sun, was it was pink like her dress.

"She's all yours," Smitty whispered, snortling uncontrollably. "Now, listen, when you slip the shoe on over her heel, slide your hand up and give her leg a squeeze."

"What?" My hands began to sweat.

He gave me a shove. "Come on. Do like I said. They expect it."

I swallowed a large amount of saliva, wiped my hands on my pants, and stumbled forward, trying to smile which she returned as she settled into the chair. On one side a tooth was missing. She wanted a white pair, she said, and could I put on a pair of rhinestone bows. I pulled up the stool and measured her foot. When I went to the wall for her size, remarkably large, Smitty gave me the nod. My shirt was wringing wet.

I returned to the stool, displayed the shoe for her approval, took out my shoehorn, and spooned her heel into the shoe. My hand would not leave the metal horn.

"Too big," she said.

I could hardly get it off and went behind a wall of boxes with Smitty following me and whispering, "For cry sake, you're treating her like your mother. Now just watch me."

He took the smaller shoe and seated himself on the stool. "He just started this morning. I think I can assist you." Taking his shoehorn, he forced her foot into the shoe and as he did so, his hand slid up her silken calf and squeezed.

Like lightning her foot flew up, caught him under the chin and flipped him backwards off the stool. She never lost her smile showing the empty socket. "I like the other kid," she said. I dived behind the walls of boxes before Smitty could pick himself up and see me watching, and when I came out again, the woman was gone, Smitty was flushed blood-red, and the Oklahoma cowboy stood inside the open double doors, laughing with the tears running down his cheeks.

Happy Town

18

As I worked day by day in the dim, stifling interior of Balster's Merc, the dam progressed. Out of the pit behind the earth fill the dust rose. Choking, soup-thick, it was stirred by the constant activity of the great cats as they crept and crawled, backed and filled across the now dry riverbed far below the bluffs. One by one the gigantic concrete buttresses began to rise in position where they would hold the growing earth fill against the someday force of that awesome river when it should be unleashed.

Returning from the dam at night, Conrad was tired, dirty, disgusted when he got home and lashed at me bitterly for being clean and for recounting lighthearted descriptions and anecdotes to get my mother to smile.

"Oh, Christ, I'm not a dirt stiff," he burst out as we settled into our bedrolls under the sky.

"You want to make a place productive," I said. "You don't want to do just the digging up part."

He was silent, and I figured he would kill me for my pity.

"Yeah, that's it, that's it." He sat up. "You know, that dam will never turn the prairie green. We were standing around today — we lean on our shovels half the time — I said that it would, and this guy just laughed in my face. I could have knocked his teeth in. He said it was just a big heap of dirt we're supposed to pile up and there isn't any reason for it. He's kind of an agitator. He's always trying to make you feel what you're doing is worthless, but the more I think about it, the more I think he's right. Where are the plans for irrigation ditches, for aqueducts and flumes? I don't think there are any. I haven't heard of them. And if you don't carry this water, well, what good is it? It'll just be a big lake behind a great big earth fill out in the middle of nowhere. What good will it do? What use? That's what I want to know, what use is it, all this dough and all the work. I hate that guy. I hate the stinking son of a bitch, but, Christ, I think he's right."

"FDR wouldn't spend all these millions and millions for nothing. Congress wouldn't do it."

"All these guys vote," Conrad said.

"Maybe he has to do something," I said. "It's pretty desperate out here."

"You can say that again."

Staring up into the sky, my arms behind my head, I felt enormous pity for Conrad. All our lives he had taken the brunt of everything, the childhood discipline, the boyhood punishments and deprivations, which had been wrong for him. I pitied him, and yet I wasn't sorry, because I had carefully stood behind him and missed the worst of it and because of him, as we lay under the stars,

I saw my world growing outward at a breathtaking rate while he muttered, "Oh, shit," in frustration.

Like my life, Deal expanded visibly outward across the plain. Men arrived, singly and in pairs, rented a lot for a couple of bucks, parked their jalopy, and dug a hole for the outhouse. After they hired on at the dam or in the bars and stores or set up shop to practice their trades as barbers or cobblers or mechanics, they knocked together a shanty of packing crates. A Swede carpenter arrived and went into the tarpaper shack business. Rumor had it, he was cleaning up a fortune. He partnered with a woman from the Klondike to build a row of apartments, so called, a desolate facade of raw lumber where a door and a window alternated with a door and a window, and the boardwalk rested flat on the prairie with the dust puffing upward through the cracks. The apartments were never empty.

Across the prairie and the river the government town also grew. In orderly rows the barracks stood along the trimmed streets, but no one wanted to live there. The careful government town was derided in Deal. "Christ, I wouldn't live there," one man told me as he bought yellow-tinged oxfords. "Every time you take a leak, you think you're doing something wrong."

"You can't say that about Deal," I said.

We hung out at night with Doc Stengel who turned out to be not a doctor but an impoverished medical student running the dispensary. When he said he gave out Band-Aids, he meant it. That tall, skinny, Abe Lincoln from Cleveland, Ohio, made the truth very funny. Several nights a week Doc Stengel had dinner with us in the tarpaper shack where we argued back and forth about the condition of the country. "This prairie makes me think of Lake Erie," Doc said, "a vast expanse of absolutely nothing."

Conrad and I stared at him across the table, and my father muttered, "It's been a bit dry here since you came."

Conrad snorted. Then for the first time when Conrad struck out against the desecrators of the prairie, I heard him say "we" instead of "they."

"We've got to live with its limits, that's all. You can't make a place what it isn't. We've got grass, but we only have so much water and a hell of a lot of sun and wind. This isn't Iowa where you come from."

"Ohio."

"All right, Ohio then, same thing."

My mother asked what Ohio looked like, and Doc said, "Rolling hills which flatten out near the big rivers and the Great Lakes. Factory towns and farms and woods covering the hills. They turn purple in the spring when the redbud blooms."

Her face lit with pleasure. "It sounds like Wisconsin where I grew up. It was so green there and shady and the woods were full of redbud."

"Maybe you should go back there, Mom," I said.

My parents stared at me, startled. I knew that wasn't the solution.

After supper we moved out on the stoop, and I gave Doc a lesson in rolling your own. Doc's long face furrowed with concentration, his nonexistent chin pressed into his skinny neck, as he bent every effort on the little white paper spilling out Bull Durham tobacco.

Day faded around us, and the long, healing twilight followed. The diamond-glitter of the first planet lost ground in the star-spread night. I could smell the dust then that lay heavily over the town, and the excavation for the dam, and I heard the night noise from the main street with great clearness. Listening to the roar of automobile motors, oo-ga honks, the jazz, shouts, the hum of voices, bursts of laughter, sometimes louder and softer as if someone played the score on a hand-pumped organ, I wondered if more occurred at night on that boardwalked main drag, or if I just heard it more clearly. It went night and day, twenty-four hours without stopping. When men came off any shift at the dam, they could have a glass of beer, a meal, a round with a taxi dancer in the long bare halls. In the daylight all the noise and movement went on within a wider context which disappeared at night, leaving only the life of bars and cafes, joints and brothels.

As we sat on the stoop, talking among ourselves, half listening, half hearing, we were irresistibly drawn toward the noise, and after a while, we moved toward Doc's dust-covered black Ford, the three of us squeezing in front on two bucket seats.

Up the main street we drove slowly past the open double doors, stopping to talk when somebody hailed us, made a U-turn at the end of the wide street, and came down the other side. We followed the street out of town toward the river.

Here a side road made a downhill loop, and along the outer edge of the curve were strung the houses of prostitution. They were the best houses in Deal. They stood firmly, without listing in the wind, and they had clapboard or carsiding exteriors; and they were painted gleaming pink and blue and white and strung with lights. The front doors stood open, and driving past we could look into the barroom where the men drank and the girls were standing, sitting on laps, talking with them. I wondered about the men inside and the degree of loneliness or lust or necessity which drew them there. The women, I supposed, had all been raped as young girls, even the tall, skinny one who lounged nude against a doorjamb.

"So this is Happy Town," Doc said. "My, my."

My laugh came out half strangled and very nervous.

We ended up in The Green Frog where we held down three stools for a couple of beers. Nobody ever asked me if I was old enough to drink. Only the laws of necessity were enforced in that town. Just being in Deal separated the men from the boys. We stayed away from the Bring 'Er Inn and, except to look, from Happy Town. There were depths where we feared to go.

The next morning I was back in the merc, my window on main street. It struck me that I was perfectly happy living in a shacktown with work and something to eat and life boiling around me. What if it was a world peopled with dirt stiffs and cat skinners, peddlers and prostitutes, churned up in wide-open, lawless existence that maintained its velocity twenty-four hours a day? Or I was almost perfectly happy, if only my mother wasn't mixed up in it. The Oklahoma cowboy came in for new work shoes.

"They was fightin' on the dam again today."

"A big one?"

"They took one guy to the hospital, had him on a stretcher. Say, you know him, the kid you was in The Green Frog with."

"That's my brother."

"About your height? Hooked nose? Kind of a swagger?"

I threw down my sales pad and ran.

Conrad sat at the kitchen table, his nostrils wadded with cotton and a blood bruise closing one eye. Doc Stengel held my mother's head down on her crossed arms. My stomach dropped away. With a shaking hand my father poured whisky from a flat pint bottle.

"My God, Conrad, what happened?"

"You know that agitator guy I told you about. I got fed up."

"You should have ducked."

"I did, right where he figured I would."

"Leave your nose alone," Doc said.

I knew it was the first fight Conrad had ever lost. I was chilled because of it.

"Drink some whisky and forget about it," my father said. "He's all right."

I stared at him.

"My God, how can you say that?" I cried out. "How can you say that?"

He didn't look at me. He was never going to face the truth, unless someone forced him.

My Father
Face-to-Face

19

The last thing my father said next morning was, "Billy, help your mother set up the washtubs," and the minute my mother was out of the kitchen, Conrad said, "I'll kill that old man. If he didn't have to wear those goddam white shirts to the motor pool every day, she wouldn't have wash up to here." Then he laughed, dry and bitter. "They're both going to die of white shirts, one naturally and the other unnaturally. I'll write his epitaph, 'He died with his white shirt on.'"

Then Doc let loose a riot of beeps on the horn out in front, and Conrad pushed aside his undrunk coffee and went with him to the dispensary.

The old wringer Maytag stood against the wall of the tarpaper house with a faded cotton blanket over it. The tubs hung on hooks on the laths which bound the sheets of building paper, and I got them down and balanced them on an old sawhorse and began the endless job of filling them, carrying teakettles and saucepans of heated water from the stove inside, trip after trip, trying to make the water something better than lukewarm. My mother came out carrying the soiled clothes in a wide wicker basket, and I felt stricken that I hadn't thought to carry it out for her. While she began sorting into piles on the earth, I continued to fill the rinse tubs, and I guess I hadn't balanced them properly on the sawhorse because as the first one reached half-full, it suddenly flipped and emptied onto the prairie.

My mother cried out. The hot water, heated with paid-for kilowatts, soaked into our shoes and swirled around the heaps of soiled clothes and turned the packed earth to mud.

"Oh, Billy," she cried, and suddenly she was weeping hysterically, horrible shuddering sobs which weren't sobs at all. She slumped down on the sawhorse and doubled over, shaking and sucking in hoarse breaths.

I stood transfixed, saying things like, "It's all right, Mom. It's just an accident. I'll fix it up." I picked up a towel from a heap to hand it to her, but it was soaked with dirty water. I picked up something else, a white shirt, and threw it viciously as far from me as I could, and got the broom and began sweeping the water away.

Gradually my mother pulled herself together, and I set up the tubs again and balanced them carefully and filled them with water and got the old Maytag going and then I left and half ran down the street. I turned around, walking backwards, waving my thumb, past whisky row almost to the other end before I hooked a ride.

The walk-in door of the motor pool garage was open, and I stepped over the threshold and into the big space with its smell of grease and monoxide. My father was seated at his desk in the far corner under the light bulb, and I walked straight toward him. I passed a truck with the hood up and the tools laid out on a grease towel on the fender and my fingers slid over them, the cool steel of wrenches, as I passed. He was seated with his back toward me in his long white mechanic's coat with the pencil-blue stripe and I could see the edge of his white collar around the back of his neck. When I was six feet from him, he turned around in his swivel chair and smiled at me and said, "Hi, Bill."

Bill, he said, not Billy. He was wearing little round steel-rimmed glasses. I had never seen them before, not on him, little old-fashioned glasses with steel wires that looped over his ears. The light gleamed on the gray metal. He looked old.

My throat worked. No words came.

"You're . . . it . . . this . . . she's . . . I . . ."

He watched me. "Are you in some kind of trouble?"

I shook my head.

"What's happening . . . what's happening . . . it's terrible . . ."

"What's happening — to *you?* What is happening?"

"No! No!"

"Calm down, son. Here, sit down on this drum. You've been working too hard and then all this galavanting at night. You need more rest, I can see that."

"No! No! I don't need any rest. That's not it. It's . . . it's . . ."

"It's what?"

"Mom! It's Mom!" The word burst like a dike inside

me, and words tumbled out, disjointed phrases, half sentences, meaningless articles, in a wild confusion even I did not understand. My father stared at me.

"You . . . it's . . . the . . . we're . . . We're killing Mom. We're killing Mom."

He turned back to the dispatcher's papers on the greasy desk.

"Is that what's on your mind?"

I nodded fiercely, as if I would strangle.

"I've been thinking about that, too, Bill. I know it."

As if the flood had turned and crashed over me, I was washed with relief. Words tumbled wildly out of me again.

"I know it, I know it. We can't stay here. It's too much for her. I've been trying to think what to do, and I think now — do you mind putting that wrench down?"

"What wrench?"

"The one in your hand. You're waving it like a maniac."

"Oh."

"I think if we can make it through the summer here, I'll have enough cash to carry us over. Then I think maybe we should all pack up and go back to Great Plain. Our roots are there, and it's a good town. They say the wool house may start up again under some new agriculture plan. That'd put a floor under us, and a roof over our heads." He smiled sadly at me, and I nodded.

Suddenly I couldn't bear it, the steel-rimmed glasses, the willingness to go back. "Yeah, but, maybe there's a better place. I mean, Great Plain isn't the only . . ."

He smiled grimly.

"I mean some place . . . Great Plain isn't the . . ."

"No. No. It's good enough for me. I'm ready to settle

228

for it. And your mother . . ." and he looked at me with a little smile. "She'd like to go back."

Outside the heat and light hit me. And the dryness. I walked through what trucks were left in the parking area until my knees almost let go and I leaned against a fender and tucked my hands under my arms to calm their trembling. After a while I moved out onto the road, but my knees refused to make it and I slumped, squatted cowboy style, against a fence post. How long I squatted there, I don't know, or what I thought about, or what I saw, or rather, what passed in front of my eyes. I just squatted against the fence post more fatigued than I had ever been in my life and after a while hungrier until a car stopped on the road in front of me and I stood up and I was staring into the face of Doc Stengel.

"Jesus," he said, "what are you doing out here? Have you got heatstroke or something?" He laid his long hand across my forehead. I stared at him, and he took my arm and pulled me into his car. "Ever have a whisky and ditch at ten A.M.? You look as if you need one, and I know I need one. Some crazy mutt got in a fight and nearly died on me, right in the dispensary. I kept telling him, you can't do that, I'm not a doctor yet. I think he was allergic to something I gave him, because he was tough as a bear and it wasn't the first fight he'd ever been in, or the worst."

We were in the middle of whisky row, and he said, "I favor The Green Frog at ten A.M. after a guy has tried to die on me. Do you have a preference?"

I said no, and we pushed into The Green Frog. It was dark and the green inside was cool and the bar was open and behind it the bartenders were ready. We sat down on the stools at the back bar and Doc said, "Two whisky and ditch, John, my friend, for two potential murderers. I almost killed a guy, and this young man is thinking seriously about it. Put your socket wrench on the bar, Catlett. Concealed weapons aren't allowed in respectable joints."

The bartender poured out the whisky and two glasses of water and leaned back across from us and asked, "Who'd you give it to this time, Doc?"

"You make it sound easy. This was a very tough case. Give me another. Ready, Billy boy? Make it two, John. Another dam accident. I had to use every trick in my bag. I didn't go to med school for nothing. It takes years to learn this stuff. This kid is getting hysterical, John, better give him another."

About noon Doc Stengel steered me down the street to his place and laid me out on the bed. Face down with my arms dangling to the floor, I slept the whole afternoon.

When he woke me, I was gummy with sweat and my clothes stuck to the coverlet and the pillow was soaked. He asked, "Feel okay?" Oddly enough, I did. He gave me a glass of water and some gum before I went out.

My father was already at home in the kitchen. He was still wearing his white shirt and tie, but he had put on his worn-out moccasins. My mother was just dishing up large bowls of chili-mac to go with the coleslaw and corn bread when I came in. The whole room smelled of chili and freshly ironed, sun-dried clothes. The white shirts hung in a neat row on a clothesline.

"Billy," my mother said, "where were you today? I've been worried sick. Mr. Balster sent word that you didn't come to work and if you don't come tomorrow, he's going to give your job to somebody else."

"Well," I said, "today I got plastered."

"Billy Catlett!" my mother shrieked. "Oh, this terrible place. It will be the ruin of us yet."

"Boys grow up, Mother." Then my father turned to me and said, "But you'd better get to work tomorrow, Bill. We need everybody's help, you know, if we're going to get out of here."

"I will," I said, noticing that he said Bill again, not Billy. "By the way, here's the wrench. I forgot to put it back."

Butterfly Boots

20

I had expected to feel free, now that my father and my mother planned to return to Great Plain, but oddly I didn't. I was no freer than before. I needed to act, to do something for myself, with myself, on my own. Nothing came my way, nor was it likely to. I would have to strike out and find it. There was a lot of the world I had never seen. If something was out there for me, I had to search for it myself. I said as much one night as Conrad and I sat around, chewing the rag, in Doc's place.

"That's the dumbest thing I ever heard of," Conrad said. "Just tell me one thing you can do. How are you going to get along? All you've ever done is punch cows and sell stuff."

"I kind of think I'll head East," I said. Conrad picked up Doc's guitar which he had ordered through Ward's catalog so he could play "Home on the Range" and tuned it. He didn't believe me.

"That's a great idea," Doc said. "When?"

"Maybe this fall, when the folks go back to Great Plain."

I threw a leg over the arm of Doc's chair.

"You're absolutely right, but that's incidental. I don't expect to punch cattle in Illinois, but I do expect to take care of myself. That's what I learned out at Sam's place and here, too, more than anything else. That's too much tobacco, Doc. Shake a little out."

"Then I'll lose it."

"You will anyway."

Conrad worked up the strings.

"What do you intend to do? You haven't a plan in your head. You're just going to stand out in the middle of the street and see what happens."

I nodded.

"He's nuts."

"Oh, I don't know," Doc said, and Conrad played a chord.

"He's been listening to our old man. All our lives he's been chasing rainbows, first this way, then that way, and he wants everybody else to do it, too. That'll make him right, see?"

"I think he's chased the last one for him."

"He's kidding you."

"He's going back to Great Plain. Just doing that is an admission."

"You wait till he's been there awhile, and he'll get that look in his eye and he'll be restless again."

"Well, maybe so. I don't mean to make a lifetime prediction, but now he's willing to go back. I guess everybody dreams a little, of striking it rich, of adventure beyond the rimrock."

"Each man to his own rainbow," Doc said, lighting up finally.

"Not me," Conrad said with scorn. "There aren't going to be any rainbows for me. I'm going to put my hands down and feel what I want. I'm going to be able to pat the piece of earth that's mine. The piece I own free and clear. The piece nobody can take away from me, where I know I can eat and work and live and be my own man. Hell, I wouldn't . . ."

"But that's your dream," Doc said. "Okay, it's not pie in the sky. It isn't a rainbow, but you don't have it yet, either. It's a very possible dream, a probable one for you, because you use what you already know a lot about in the place you already know, but that's not all of it, Connie." He was the only man to get away with calling him Connie to his face. "It takes money to get land and get machinery and good breeding stock. How do you plan to do that without a debt in the world?"

"Just what I'm doing."

Doc and I watched him.

"Just what I'm doing is what I plan to do. I'm going to make every nickel out of this dam that I can. This dam is going to turn the prairie green again, but not the way we thought when we came up here. When I've got the biggest grubstake I can make and the place I have my eye on opens up, then I'm going to jump, and I'll make the greenest little patch of prairie you ever did see."

Doc turned to me and said, "Your brother is a very practical dreamer," and I grinned. It was the greatest idea I ever heard.

"How about that?" Conrad said. "See what I mean?"

"All right. You want to live and work on the land.

That's the kind of life you want, and it sounds great —
for you. It isn't a better life than the one Bill may want,
and it isn't worse, either. It's your kind, and you're
damn lucky to know it, but as soon as you start cram-
ming it down somebody else's throat, you are doing
what you say your father has done, trying to get everybody to live his way because that makes him right."

Conrad picked up the guitar again and hit the melody
of "My Little Girl." Looking at me, he laughed. "Doc's
right. Still I can see you, lugging those sample cases up
the veranda of the Laurel, trying to get in on the
ground floor of something that's going to be big." He
sang another line: ". . . a thousand miles from home."

He made me a little sore. "Maybe I will end up
lugging sample cases into the Laurel. Or maybe I'll
come back and hoe my own pea patch. I don't know yet,
but if I do, I want to be able to say I took a look at the
world and made my choice. Chicago's only my first
stop."

"Burbank got to you." Conrad's face, stuffed nose and
all, brightened. "Say. I forgot about the Mitchell girl. Is
she still going to school back there?"

I shrugged. "Could be." Would I ever reach the point
where I could be open with Conrad?

"Well, well. Now how're we going to launch this kid
on his life of adventure? Which way did you say you
were going?"

"East."

"I'll bet I've seen more rainbows in the eastern sky
than I've seen in the West."

He couldn't let go without a few jabs.

"First I'm going to help the folks get back to Great
Plain. I can't go anywhere before that."

"What about money?" Doc said.

"I have a nice roll."

"You can hitchhike. But that's not so good going East. There's the train. Day coach wouldn't be much."

"Maybe I could hire on a cattle train."

Conrad lit up. "There you've got it. Bill here's an old puncher by trade. He trod the boards for many years in the role of cowboy."

There was a limit to the jabbing I could take, and we were fast approaching it. He strummed a few soothing chords.

"What about Kincaid's?" I said.

"Kincaid's is sure to be shipping. I'll write Jim tonight. You can go as far as Chicago and have a free ride back if things don't pan out, and the first adventure that comes along you can skip freight."

"Brilliant solution," Doc said. "Absolutely brilliant."

Conrad ran through, "Oh, little girl, tum-tum-ta-ta-ta, a thousand miles from home." Doc and I smoked in silence.

"You know," I said. "I guess everybody sets up some objective for himself, everybody I know, anyway, except for one man. I've only known one man in all my life who took it as it came, or seemed to, and that was Seth McCollum."

"Who is he?" Doc said.

"He isn't, but he was." When I finished telling him about Seth, Doc was silent. Then he nodded several times.

My last day in the merc I leaned against the merchandise counter directly under the paddle fan which stirred the hot air. A rangy, newly sunburned man entered and looked over the shoes before he saw me and spoke, "I want some boots."

"Work boots?"

"Cowboy boots."

"If you're thinking of working in them, they aren't too good for walking around. They're designed for . . ."

"Cowboy boots," he said.

I showed him to a chair and pulled up the stool and measured his foot. I looked into his face then, into the burned blue eyes. They flicked across the pots and pans counter. What was he doing buying useless cowboy boots, when most likely he needed to send the money home? I went into the alleys of shoe boxes and found the pair embroidered with butterflies. They cost so much that he had to change his mind.

Seated again on the stool I opened the box and held up those magnificent boots. I turned the butterflies this way and that in the dim light and watched his face soften, the reddened eyes brighten.

"I'll try 'em," he said.

Pushing and pulling, I managed to cram his foot inside. Obviously he had never had a pair before. He was from Detroit, he told me, and his family was still back there.

"Things pretty bad?"

"There isn't much work. A man's got to work." He ran his hand over the intricate toolings of the leather. "A man's got to work."

And live and dream a little, I thought, saying, "They're twenty-eight fifty."

He asked, "Can I put them on layaway? A dollar down and a dollar a week until I've paid for them?" I nodded.

Even in wide-open Deal I hadn't found anyone who looked the whole naked business straight in the eye. Doc came closest, maybe, but he got it down with laughter. The rest of them fooled themselves with something, drink or money or dreams, right up to the terrible moment when they could fool themselves no longer.

Cattle Train to Beyond

21

Early in September we left Deal, crossed the barren, sheep-scattered plateau, and descended again toward the confluence of the Yellowstone and the Honey rivers. Great Plain was still there. The place was so wonderfully familiar that I had to laugh out loud, and, riding the truck bed standing, I felt like a returning hero, a soldier who has seen the front and lived to tell about it.

Since no renters had come along in our absence, we moved back into the old four-square house and gathered in the kitchen for a final lunch. Conrad seated our lady mother without being told, and my father spread his napkin, saying, "It may be a long time before we're together again. We'll clasp hands."

Our joined hands circled the old round table.

"O Lord," he said, "bless and watch over these, thy wanderers." He suddenly stopped, looked down, and said an abrupt amen.

Afterwards my mother put together two lunches, one

for Conrad to take back to Deal when he returned the borrowed truck and set up housekeeping with Doc, the other for me to take aboard the cattle train.

"Do you have enough money, Bill?" my father said.

"One hundred and fifty dollars," I said, and I was very proud of it.

"And you have your return coach ticket, if you need it?"

I slapped my breast pocket. The free return trip was part of the pay for a cowpuncher who rode to the stockyards of the great Middle Western cities.

"I know you have to go," my mother said, and she smiled chin up with tears flooding behind her glasses.

"I'm not going off the edge of the world," I laughed, hugging her and knowing that in a way I was. My father shook hands with me and whispered, "Good luck, son." I looked back and waved, and they waved, until the truck rounded the corner and they were out of sight.

For a minute I wondered if I should go, and I looked at Conrad. He was busy driving with his eyes fixed straight ahead.

The mooing and bellering and dust filled the part of town around the stockyards with such sweet familiar sounds and smells that my spirits soared again. I saw in a glance that the pens were not full. This year's had not been a big drive, and I knew without thinking what it meant in hardships past and to come. Beyond the crisscross pattern of pens and walkways the cattle cars stood on the siding. The great doors were slid open. The cleated ramps were in place, and beside each door stood the tally man with his sheaf of papers. In the great pen mounted cowboys drove the cattle into the chutes where men on foot punched them to keep them moving toward the ramp. Other men hung to the sides of the slatted cars and prodded the cattle into the ends. The whooping and hollering, the swinging ropes, the smack of hemp on hide, the dust and animal smell rose with the bellering and filled the air.

Tom was riding in the pen nearest the chute. He was mounted on his favorite little cow pony, the one that knew as much about the business of herding and cutting as any cowboy alive, and Tom rode him in his usual light manner. Tom drove the herd back and forth until the last critter entered the chute leading to the ramp, and I quickly jumped off the fence and closed the gate. Tom grinned at me, swinging off his horse, and I grinned back.

"Long time no see, Pistol," he said. We shook hands and he offered me the makings. Standing in the pen, we rolled and licked little damp cigarettes and lit up with stove matches.

"Where've you been?" Tom said.

I told him about the dam, and with the reins looped over his arm, he listened, squinting at me keenly from time to time. When I finished, Tom said, "I made a few changes myself. I got married."

My mouth dropped. "Who to?"

"Lacey Barnett."

He grinned. "It's better than booze," he said.

I knew what he meant. Like calling a tremendous blizzard a little snow underfoot.

"Are you still on the same place?" I asked.

Tom shook his head. "I'm renting up the Mizpah."

"Is Sam around?"

"He never came back, Pistol. His place is up for sale."

Someone was shouting. "Driscoll, your papers are

ready to sign," and he tied his little horse to the rail. We shook hands and parted, Tom making his way to the tally man near the door. Just to see him sober and on his horse and working his cattle made me feel good, and I smiled inside over the conversation with its spare words and its volumes of unstated information.

Conrad met me in the walkway. "I saw Jim Kincaid. You're all set."

Red brushed past us, looking at me twice before he recognized me and then instead of greeting me, he clapped me on the shoulder with his big brown paw and said, "That son of a bitch Diller, this time I'm goin' to kill him," and went on.

Taking my Gladstone bag and my bedroll and checking my money, I shook hands with Conrad. Neither of us spoke. I began to move away before he said, "Good luck, buddy."

"Good luck, Conrad."

"Hang onto your day coach ticket."

I grinned. "Don't worry."

"There are worse places than this one."

"I just want to find out for sure," I said.

The old Pullman, painted a shiny railroad red, was so ancient that it had colored glass in the fan windows. Leading with my bedroll, I mounted the steps under the canopy and pushed into the car, past the men's room and the washbasin and the water cooler and the long table, also a shiny railroad red, and the black cookstove with the coal bin, to the other end of the car where the ancient red plush Pullman seats had been folded out and stretched against the wall. The bunks, a bedroll wide, filled two-thirds of the car, making room for a dozen punchers, some of whom had already taken pos-

242

session of a space by a bedroll or a suitcase. Selecting an empty one, I threw my bedroll into the baggage rack above and pushed my Gladstone under the seat. Turning, I saw Fonse. He watched me from the opposite bank of seats, his knees crossed, one small booted foot dangling, and a half-smoked wet, crimped cigarette cupped in his hand.

"Howdy, Pistol," he said.

I wanted to laugh. He sounded as if he had seen me day before yesterday, not year before last. "Goin' someplace?"

"I'm thinking about it."

He nodded.

The men drifted in, after having gone up town to clean up at the Marshall House. The trail drive beards were gone with the sweat-stained shirts and the dirty Levi's. Someone shouted, "Give a hand here." I jumped up and went to the door and took the rope handle of the huge chuck box marked Kincaid Cattle Company in black letters. I wondered who was to do the cooking on the long haul east until I saw Greasy Granger weaving his way through the crowd. He had a large paper bag in his arms, which, when he tried to get through the door, suddenly split from bottom to top. He fell to his knees as the fifths of Sunnybrook tumbled out.

A yell went up. "Now we're ready," and "Come on, engineer, we've got everythin'. What're you waitin' for?"

The first jerk forward spilled Greasy in the aisle, and the curses filled the car. "That wooden Indian! He just took ten pounds off the best beef in Montana."

A series of jars hit the Pullman. Out the half-open windows the punchers stuck their heads and whooped and hollered. "Aw, come on, Suzie, we got room."

"Be good," a ranch woman hollered back.

"Don't do anything I wouldn't do," hollered Conrad, bringing on deafening whoops and cowboy yells.

"Don't get lost in the big city."

"Don't take any wooden nickels."

Grinding and jerking, with head-snapping jars and humps the great engine gathered steam. Accompanied by bellering and cowboy yells, the cattle train moved east.

The train had not gathered full speed before hats were hung on the light fixtures and clothes hooks, and the men gathered in the three or four berths still left upright, the seats at right angles to the length of the car with shiny tables hooked into slots. Cards appeared, the Sunnybrook was unstoppered, and Fonse said, "Deal."

Greasy Granger stoked the cookstove with coal, lit the fire with the oily string waste from the railway cars' wheel boxes, and began to heat up the cooking fires in the already steaming car.

I stepped outside under the canopy of the old Pullman. The crack of wheels on rails came through the metal floor. I leaned out the open upper section of the door and gazed across the bone dry prairie. The distant hills, ridges, outcroppings, the conical forms, the spreading buttes, returned to three dimensions in the lowering light. Close at hand the even, regularly spaced ends of ties sped beneath my feet, the clumps of silver sage, dry and odorless, wheeled forward in the curious way of stationary objects observed at great speed.

Opening the lower part of the door, I reached around to the iron rungs whch made a ladder up the side of the car. I did not look down. I did not think down. I found a toehold. The sickening sensation of exposure and

244

speed and frailty threatened to capture me. Hand over hand, feeling with my toes, never looking for the rung for my feet, I climbed to the car roof. Along the center ran a level walkway for the punchers to get to the cattle cars while the train was in motion. No one else was on top. It was too early yet. The stock didn't need anything and would not be fatigued enough to lie down and require a punch to get them up again before they were trampled.

I pulled my hat down against the wind, and sat down on the level path. Little pellets of soot stung my cheek.

From my perch I could see the long string of cattle cars and beyond the steaming engine the parallel steel rails racing to the horizon. The rails seemed to spring again out the rear of the car and trail away to the western line where the town of my boyhood had already disappeared.

What lay ahead I had no idea. I had never seen another place, smelled other smells, known other people, another life. The glittering strings of steel carried me beyond the horizon of my knowledge.

I pulled up my knees and rested my chin on my crossed arms, and looking off across the prairie, I smiled to myself. Excitement caught in my lungs.

That was September 1934.